SEDUCING HIS FATE

Predator Peak

Book 2

ELENA AITKEN

E.R. AITKEN

Needing Happily Ever After

Wanting Happily Ever After

Fighting Happily Ever After

We Wish You A Happily Ever After

Keeping Happily Ever After

Finding Happily Ever After

Seeking Happily Ever After

Cherishing Happily Ever After

Ever After: Volume One (Books 1-4)

The Springs Series

Summer of Change

Falling Into Forever

Second Glances

Winter's Burn

Midnight Springs

She's Making A List

Summit of Desire

Summit of Seduction

Summit of Passion

Fighting For Forever

The Springs Collection: Volume 1

The Springs Collection: Volume 2

The Springs Collection: Volume 3

The Springs Complete Collection - Books 1-10

Destination Paradise

Shelter by the Sea

Escape to the Sun

Hidden in the Sand

The McCormicks

Love in the Moment

Only for a Moment

One more Moment

In this Moment

From this Moment

Our Perfect Moment

The McCormicks: Volume One

The McCormicks: Volume Two

Finally Series

Finally Yours

Finally Mine

Finally Fell

Finally Forever

Finally Free

Vegas

Nothing Stays in Vegas

Return to Vegas

Timber Creek

When We Left

When We Were Us

When We Began

When We Fell

Timber Creek: The Complete Series

Castle Mountain Lodge

Unexpected Gifts

Hidden Gifts

Unexpected Endings - Short Story

Mistaken Gifts

Secret Gifts

Goodbye Gifts

Tempting Gifts

Holiday Gifts

Promised Gifts

Accidental Gifts

The Castle Mountain Lodge Collection: Books 1-3

The Castle Mountain Lodge Collection: Books 4-6

The Castle Mountain Lodge Collection: Books 7-9

The Castle Mountain Lodge Complete Collection

Stand Alone Stories

All We Never Knew

Drawing Free

Composing Myself

Betty & Veronica

Halfway Series

Halfway to Nowhere

Halfway in Between

Halfway to Christmas

Chapter One

THE LIGHT WAS WRONG. It was too dark and there was a weird shadow over her right eye.

Dakota Hill took one more look around the living room that she'd converted into a temporary studio and adjusted the ring light to give her better lighting, but it still wasn't quite right. She needed daylight. Her eyes flicked to the picture windows at the back of the room. She generally had the heavy curtains pulled open wide to the wild forest behind her small house. One of the perks of living in Predator Peak in the remote Canadian Rockies was that she was surrounded by trees, mountains, and wilderness. As far north as they were, there were a lot more trees than people. Just the way she liked it.

But instead of looking out over the forested area behind her house the way she usually preferred, Dakota had the curtains pulled closed. In fact, every window covering in the house had been buttoned up tight for the last little while. It was safer that way.

Even if she hated every second of it.

And it definitely didn't help her with her current lighting situation.

Once more, Dakota sat at the table she'd set up with her laptop, a mirror, and her makeup supplies. The shadow was still there, but she was going to have to live with it. She was out of time.

With a deep breath, Dakota leaned forward and clicked a few buttons on her laptop. The green light that indicated her camera was on flashed for a moment and then glowed solid. She took a moment to check the shot on the screen. She made a few slight adjustments until she was satisfied that only her left eye was in the camera shot.

Only once she was happy with the angles did she click the button that set her broadcast to public. And just like that, she was live on social media.

"Hello, lovelies," she purred into her microphone, keeping her voice low and soft despite the fact that the voice her viewers heard wasn't hers at all. Dakota used a voice filter to further soften the edges of her voice to a melodic, overall pleasing, almost hypnotic tone.

"Thank you for joining me today," she continued. "You're live with Fuchsia." Her *influencer* name rolled off her tongue. "I'm so glad you're here with me" Her gaze flickered down to the corner where she could see the number of people watching her feed. The number was multiplying quickly, but she knew from experience that she needed a few minutes of chatter before she could get into the technique of the day. She filled the time by telling a cute and completely made-up story about how she'd ordered a latte at Starbucks earlier that day and the barista had mixed up her order. There were no chain restaurants of any kind within hours of Predator Peak, but that little detail wasn't important.

Her followers enjoyed hearing little slice-of-life stories about her day-to-day activities. Even if they were totally fiction. And they were. The life that Fuchsia led was much more exciting than Dakota's reality. But no one needed to know that as long as she wasn't hurting anyone with her little white lies.

All she needed to do was keep coming up with unique makeup looks, and easy-to-follow tutorials for the more basic ones, and her followers would be happy. Even if she would have preferred to be more open and honest about...well, everything. It wasn't always about what *she* wanted. She'd learned that early on.

She glanced one more time at the number of followers. "Okay, everyone," she purred into the microphone, satisfied with the number of live viewers. "I think we're ready to get started today. I think you're really going to like today's look." She winked slowly into the camera before she got going.

Even a year ago, if someone would have told her that she would be a makeup influencer—on social media, of all things —there was no way she would have believed them. More likely, she would have checked for a hidden camera and the assumption that she was on some kind of prank show. Growing up, she'd never been into makeup. Not the way she was now. The dramatic and sometimes wild looks she created now would not have been tolerated when she was younger.

Presentation was important, and there was a certain expectation about how she presented herself. As the only daughter of the King family dynasty, those expectations were very, very high.

At first, she'd learned enough basic makeup techniques to satisfy her father that she wouldn't embarrass him at the many, many functions where he paraded her around as the *princess* he seemed to think she was. But over time, she started to experiment with different techniques, including some wilder and much flashier looks that she would never dare to wear outside of her room. It wasn't until she'd left the city and all the prying eyes who were always watching her every move that she allowed herself more freedom with her look. And then, as luck would have it, the world of social media allowed her to actually make money with her hobby.

Dakota kept up a steady stream of chatter as she walked her followers through the eyeshadow technique, careful to only keep her eye in the camera shot. At one point, she stopped to adjust herself a little, centering her eye. She'd become pretty good at finding the right angle, so the shot was interesting enough but also maintained her privacy. It was imperative that her privacy was maintained above all.

The fact that she'd even dared to put herself out there so publicly when her situation was so tenuous was riskier than she would have liked, but with her back against the wall, Dakota needed to provide for herself. There hadn't been a lot of options. She did what she had to.

"Okay, lovelies. I think that's it for today." Dakota blinked slowly and lowered her eyelid for her viewers to get the full effect of what she'd created. "If you have any questions, be sure to type them in, and I'll address them in a follow-up post."

She didn't usually like to stay on camera while she answered questions because she had less control and there was a greater chance that she would slip up and expose herself. As much as she craved a deeper connection with them, it just wasn't possible. At least not yet. Maybe not ever.

"Be sure to check the links I'm going to post under this video for all the amazing products I used in today's look. Stay beautiful, lovelies. I appreciate each and every one of you. I'll talk to you all soon."

Dakota signed off, making sure the camera on her laptop was covered before she sat back and exhaled.

Before she clicked off her social media profile, she peeked at the comments.

"Beautiful. I love you."

"You're the best."

"Thank you. My daughter loves you."

"Can we be best friends?"

She got her share of negative comments, too, but Dakota didn't let those bother her. Nothing a stranger on the other side of a computer screen could say to her would be nearly as hurtful as what she'd endured in her real life.

It was better to focus on all those who loved her.

Only it was Fuchsia they loved. Not her.

The smile slipped from her lips as Dakota closed the top of her laptop, stood, and stretched her long, toned arms over her head. Her muscles ached from lack of use. It had been too long since she'd allowed herself to shift and let her cougar take over.

She looked around her empty house. With all the curtains closed, it felt more like a prison than the refuge it had once been.

Dakota wrapped her arms around her waist and gave herself a squeeze as the loneliness and fear settled over her the way it always did when the cameras were off.

Her house was dark. But Konner Stark knew without getting any closer that she was in there. And he was not getting any closer. He'd almost been noticed a few times already, and the last thing he needed was to get caught.

Especially before he figured out what the hell he was going to do about Dakota Hill.

And he had absolutely *no* idea what that was going to be. From the moment Konner had set foot in Predator Peak for the first time a little over a month ago, he'd known he was in trouble. But he'd had no idea just how much until he saw her for the first time.

Trouble didn't even begin to describe the situation Konner had found himself in.

Konner slipped behind a tree and moved around to the back of the houses on the short street that Dakota lived on. There was still a good layer of snow on the ground, even in April, and Konner was careful not to leave any fresh prints. It had been years since he'd ventured out of Vancouver, and he wasn't used to the lingering winter of the Northern Canadian mountains. When he'd left the coast, buds were already popping out on the trees and the daffodils were blooming. In Predator Peak, there were no indications that spring would ever arrive.

Konner had spent his whole life in the big city of Vancouver, only occasionally heading out of town to let their bears run in the surrounding woods. But even then, those trips were far and few between. His mother had spent the majority of her life working to provide for him and his younger sister. And pay off his father's gambling debts. Truth be told, that was what Tess really worked for. Between her tailoring and alteration business and cleaning homes in the evenings and on weekends, Konner didn't know anyone to ever work so hard and never get ahead. In fact, it always seemed to be the opposite.

Every time it looked like they might have enough money to get a birthday present or maybe even a Christmas gift, Konner's father, Teddy, would have the brilliant idea that he could double their money to buy them even more gifts. A few hours later, without fail, he'd come home from the casino with a fresh black eye, or maybe a broken arm. He'd beg his wife for forgiveness, groveling at her feet to help him out of his mess *just one more time.* It sickened Konner to watch his mother —after a full day of work—get up from the chair, having just sat down for what was probably the first time all day. He'd beg her not to go. And then, when he was older, he'd offer to go in her place. But she'd never let him. Instead, his mother would silently pull her coat on, and slip her purse through her arm no matter what time of night it was, in any weather, and she'd make the trip downtown to King Casino, where she'd make a deal.

There was no way Konner could know exactly what those deals entailed, and he didn't want to. But he had a pretty good idea. Eight years ago, Teddy had finally worked himself into a hole that he wouldn't be able to get out of. When he hadn't come home that night, Konner knew in his gut what had happened. This time, before his mother found out, a twenty-year-old Konner went to the casino and spoke with Javier King himself. The debt would be too much for his mother to handle. She would crumble under the weight of it, and Konner knew it. So he'd offered up himself.

As a black bear shifter, he was big, strong, and intimidating enough to handle all of King's dirty work. It went against everything in his nature to do it. But with little choice, and his mother and little sister to protect, Konner did the only thing he could. He'd indentured himself to the mountain lion Mafia family. Over the last eight years, he'd seen more than he'd cared to and done things that he couldn't let himself dwell on, but it would all be over soon.

He had one more job, and he was free. His family would be safe, and he could move on.

It should have been a fairly easy one: find the entitled, spoiled brat of a Mafia princess who'd skipped out on her wedding, and bring her home to Daddy and her equally entitled, shitty husband-to-be.

One and done.

Konner had never met the princess. King had done a good job keeping his family away from the dirtier side of his business, which was most of it. Konner had caught glimpses of her once or twice over the years: dressed in designer clothes, looking as if she'd just stepped out of a salon where she'd spent the day—she probably had—her nose in the air, looking down on everyone else.

He had no idea why she'd run off on her fiancé, but he could guess it was for attention. He'd happily return her to King's castle and her soft, spoiled life.

When King gave him his final assignment, the one that would end their relationship once and for all, Konner went after it with extra enthusiasm. It hadn't taken long to track Angelica—even her name was pretentious—King to the back-woods town of Predator Peak. He had to give her props, though: she'd done a good job in hiding in plain sight. She'd changed her name to Dakota Hill, and she'd figured out how to make a living as a *makeup influencer*. What did that even mean? It was definitely the job of an entitled brat princess who had no actual marketable skills. He shouldn't have been surprised.

But he had been surprised. *Very* surprised.

He'd expected her to be beautiful—even from a distance, under all the makeup and fancy clothes, he could tell she was pretty. What he hadn't expected—no, what he hadn't even *considered*—was that the first time he saw her outside the local pub, the breath would be sucked from his lungs. Just a glimpse of her had sent something inside him into a frenzy, making it hard to move, to think—*hell*, making it hard to breathe.

No, he hadn't expected that at all.

After that, Konner retreated. He'd traveled to a nearby town, needing some space to think about what it meant. But it could only mean one thing, and there was no way it was even possible. She was a mountain lion; he was a bear. Fated mates? It shouldn't be possible, for so many reasons. But it became impossible to stay away. The pain of being apart from her increased every second he couldn't see her. His bear fought him until, finally, he relented and returned to Predator Peak.

He'd only been back for a few weeks, but he still refused to let himself get too close. He followed her, keeping a safe distance. He didn't know how his bear would react if he got close enough to really inhale her delicious scent of caramel and chai that he'd caught on the air when the breeze was just right. It was an intoxicating combination he would deny himself of for as long as possible.

Her behavior had changed since he'd come back to town. Konner knew he must have slipped up somewhere along the line, and she was on to him. She looked over her shoulder, she kept her blinds drawn when she was at home, and she usually didn't walk outside unaccompanied, especially once the sun set. She was scared.

He hated the fact that he was the cause of that fear. She was a cougar shifter. She shouldn't be scared of anyone. She should be fierce and formidable. But she was hiding. *Why?*

Konner couldn't allow himself to consider the fact that there was a different reason than the one he'd considered for why she was in hiding. That would complicate everything. Especially when she hadn't seemed to react to his presence the way he had to her. But maybe that was because she didn't know he was there? *What if…*

No.

He didn't have the luxury to entertain any other option besides returning her to her father and fiancé, earning his freedom and moving on.

The spoiled Mafia princess was his family's ticket to a future free of King.

To hell with fate.

No matter what his bear thought was going to happen between them, there was no way it could. Konner would make damn sure of that.

Chapter Two

"HOW ARE YOU FEELING?"

Dakota eyed up the growing belly of her best friend, Ivy. She was only six months pregnant, but as far as Dakota was concerned, Ivy looked like she could pop any day.

"I feel great." Her friend ran her hands over her swollen stomach. "I'm not even that big yet." Dakota raised an eyebrow, and Ivy laughed. "I'm not. Really. I have a feeling we're going to see some big changes in the next few months as this baby really starts growing."

Dakota shook her head and looked away. As subtly as she could, she flicked her gaze around the wooded path they were walking on. She didn't want to worry her friend. She loved their walks every few days. It was the only opportunity she had to catch up with her best friend lately, and Ivy was going to find herself with a whole lot less free time when the baby came. And of course, it didn't hurt her to get out of her house for some fresh air. Especially when Dakota knew she was just being paranoid. There was nothing to be afraid of. She was safe in Predator Peak.

Wasn't she?

Truthfully, there was no reason to believe she wasn't safe. But the feeling that she was being watched over the last month or so was starting to make her crazy, and that was almost worse than running away again. She was strong, she was fierce—at least in theory. She hadn't felt that way in a very long time, if ever. But certainly, if she had to, she could defend herself. Right?

Besides, there wasn't anyone following her. She had to believe that. Because if someone was following her, they would have made their move already.

Wouldn't they?

"Are *you* okay?" Ivy had stopped walking and stared at her, her arms crossed and resting on her belly.

The easiest thing to do would be to lie, but something told her that Ivy would see right through any bullshit she could try to blow her way. Ever since the night Dakota freaked out and called Ivy when was out of town because she'd been so sure there was someone outside her window and she had no one else to turn to, Ivy and her mate Nolan had been keeping a much closer eye on her.

In fact, it seemed like everyone in town was. More likely than not, the reason Dakota felt like she was being followed was that almost everyone she even remotely knew was keeping watch on her to make sure that she was okay. They probably all thought she was insane, or at least legitimately on her way to losing her mind, because there was no real risk. Not after so long.

She was safe.

She had to believe that.

"I'm fine." Dakota shrugged in a way that she hoped came off as casual, but Ivy clearly wasn't fooled.

"Oh yeah." She rolled her eyes. "You seem really *fine.*" Ivy softened her expression and reached for Dakota's hand. "Seriously, I worry about you."

"You shouldn't." Dakota shook off her friend's touch. It wasn't that she didn't appreciate Ivy's concern; she just didn't need it. She was also completely unused to it. As a mountain lion shifter, Dakota preferred to be alone. It wasn't that she was *prickly* or *aloof* or *snobby*, which was what most of the girls growing up thought of her; she just genuinely preferred to be alone. Most of the time.

She was an introvert. It was in her nature, as well as her nurture. Growing up as the *princess*—a term she hated—of the King Mafia, there was no room for friends or quality relationships of any kind. Her peers were either terrified of her or thought she was a stuck-up bitch. The few people who even attempted to befriend her were subject to extensive background checks for both them and their families. There weren't a lot of twelve-year-olds who thought her friendship was worth that type of scrutiny. And as she got older, no boys even bothered.

Ivy was her first real friend, and despite the fact that she was totally new to the entire concept of friendship, Dakota did value it. Which was why she shook her head and reached for both of Ivy's hands. "I'm sorry," she said. "I do appreciate your concern, and I'm so sorry that I freaked out that night and worried you in any way. I was just overtired, and the shadows got to me. Really, there was nothing and *is* nothing to worry about. I promise I'd tell you."

It was a lie, but Dakota knew if she delivered it with a soft purr, her wolf-shifter friend might be convinced. Especially considering as much as Ivy did care about her, she had bigger things to occupy her. Like a new mate and a baby on the way.

"Promise?"

She couldn't worry Ivy anymore by telling her that the fear of being followed was no longer the only thing she needed to worry about after Fuchsia received a particularly disturbing message in her inbox earlier that day.

I think I know who you are.

She didn't recognize the name of the sender and she'd been so spooked by it, she'd deleted it as soon as she read it. It was a gut reaction, and maybe not the smartest move, but more likely than not, whoever sent it was just a creep trying to scare her. There was never any foundation to messages like that and it definitely wasn't the first time she'd received one. Still, it bothered her.

Dakota batted her eyelashes and let her lips curl up into a smile that she genuinely hoped convinced her friend she was okay. "I promise."

For a moment, she was sure Ivy was going to protest again, but ultimately her friend grinned and pulled her in for a hug. "Let's go to Snowdrift," she said when she released her from the embrace. "I know I can't drink the coffee, but I can stand there and inhale and that's better than nothing."

Dakota laughed and let Ivy link her arm through hers as she led the way.

She might not be used to having a good friend, but Dakota was very quickly becoming accustomed to the warm friendship, even if she couldn't tell Ivy the truth about everything. She couldn't tell anyone. She'd risked it all by running away from her old life the way she had, but there'd been no other choice. Just like there was no choice when it came to letting anyone in on the truth. If her family ever found her...well, she couldn't bear to think about what it would mean. Icy fear ran through her at the thought of what would happen.

"You're shivering." Ivy pulled her tight into her side. "Let's get you warmed up."

As she let her friend lead her into town, Dakota pushed the negative thoughts out of her head. If her father wanted to find her, he would have already done it. She was safe. She had to believe that.

From the limited time Konner had spent in Predator Peak, he'd been able to assess a few things. It was a town full of drifters, rogues, and outcasts of all kinds. From what he could tell, most of the residents were shifters of some kind, with a few humans who either knew about the heavy shifter population and didn't care or who were oblivious to it. Either way, the townspeople appeared to value their privacy, which suited him just fine because it kept them from asking too many questions about him and who he was. His cover story as an author working on his latest thriller novel had been a good one. Especially considering he was actually working on a novel. Sure, it was the same one he'd been working on for the last three or four years, but it was hard to find time to write about a Mafia errand boy when he was busy actually being one.

Konner lifted the black coffee to his face and inhaled deeply before taking a sip. It was a strong dark roast. Just the way he liked it. None of those ridiculous fancy lattes or frothy whipped toppings and flavored syrups for him. Just a steady stream of caffeine. The stronger the better.

Since he'd discovered that Snowdrift, the café in town, would brew him a made-to-order strong pot of coffee, Konner had spent more and more time tucked into the back corner where he could keep an eye on the small café and the window outside, and have his back to the wall. He'd spent too long watching his back to leave it exposed to a room of strangers, particularly when there were so many unpredictable shifters in the crowd. Besides, this way no one could read over his shoulder to see what he was working on.

Konner's book project had not only been the perfect cover while he was in town but an excellent distraction, too. He'd become pretty skilled at avoiding phone calls, texts, and emails from the boss. So far, Konner had used every excuse he could think of as to why he hadn't found Angelica yet.

> I'm close.
>
> It was the wrong woman.
>
> I just missed her.
>
> Bad information.
>
> Any day now.

King had been patient up till now, but ironically it wasn't his boss he was concerned about. Sure, the man wanted his daughter home safe and sound, but only so he could marry her off to Dominic and unite the two Mafia families once and for all. From what Konner could tell, there was no affection between father and daughter at all. If he wasn't convinced Angelica was a spoiled little rich kid, he'd almost feel bad for her. Especially because, from his limited experience, her fiancé was a sadistic asshole just like her father. He'd seen firsthand the cold, callous way Javier King dealt with his business. The King family were definitely no innocents, but they looked positively saintly next to the family she was about to marry into.

Konner had no illusions that it was anything but an arranged marriage. For the life of him, he couldn't imagine what the girl was getting out of it, except maybe a wealthy husband so she could continue to enjoy her life of luxury. It must be worth it to agree to such an arrangement, because the man himself was absolutely horrible. Then again, maybe there was a reason other than the one King had given for why Angelica had run off.

Not that it mattered. He couldn't *let* it matter. He had a job to do. That was the only thing he was concerned with.

Konner scrubbed a hand over his face and tried again to focus on the matter at hand.

He would be returning the girl to her father. And soon. It was the only way he and his family would be able to move on once and for all. He'd been dreaming of moving his mother and sister away from Vancouver to start fresh. Maybe the Maritimes of Canada, or even a new country altogether? Somewhere where no one knew them. They deserved that. Which was why he needed to finish this job as soon as he could and start making plans.

So why was he hesitating?

His bear rumbled, and Konner swallowed hard, refusing to acknowledge his animal. Because that's all it was. An animal. He was a bear shifter and that afforded him incredible strength and size—not to mention the healing powers that had saved his ass more than once—and he took full advantage of those powers. But as far as his animal and his instincts were concerned, it was nothing but a pain in the ass. Especially lately.

Something about the woman had awoken his bear and that scared the hell out of him. Because if his reaction meant what he was sure it meant, it was going to make everything harder.

Harder. But not impossible.

He'd finish the job. He'd deliver the girl to her father and fiancé and save his own family. That's all that mattered.

Konner clenched his jaw, solidifying his resolve. Enough was enough. He couldn't put it off forever. He picked up his phone, ready to tap a response to King's latest inquiry. His fingers hovered over the keys. All he had to do was let his boss know he'd located her and was working on an extraction plan.

Simple.

He stared at the screen for another minute before clicking it off and putting his phone facedown on the table.

Fuck.

Maybe it could wait another day?

He took a deep swallow of coffee and opened his manuscript once more, losing himself in the words.

———

He knew the moment she walked in the door.

The scent of caramel and chai permeated the already thick smell of fresh coffee in the air and hit him in the gut. He sat up with a jerk, his project forgotten as his eyes locked onto the target of his every waking thought.

She had her back to him. Her long, copper hair hung down her back, perfectly straight and she stood taller than her friend, who was also tall. But where her friend was curvy with muscles and an obviously pregnant belly, *she* was lean. She moved gracefully, like a dancer, but from his intel, Konner knew she wasn't.

She didn't see him, but he watched as her back stiffened. *Did she sense him? Could she scent him the way he could her? What did he smell like to her? Would she be drawn to him in the same way?* She was a cat, and he was a bear. Konner didn't know much about how any of it worked, let alone when it came to a bear and a cat combination. Hell, it *shouldn't* work at all.

Yet here he was.

And fuck, did it ever work.

Every cell in his body pulsed with the need to go to her, pull her into his arms, and claim her as his own. His cock thickened in his pants at the idea of having her and marking her as his. It was one thing to see her at a distance, but up close? This was entirely uncharted territory.

Konner watched as she leaned toward her friend and said something in her ear before turning toward the door. *Was she leaving?*

No.

He couldn't let her leave. Not before he looked into her

eyes. With a primal urge, he needed to know whether she was feeling what he was. Konner shoved his chair back roughly on the hardwood floor. But he moved too quickly, and his leg hit the small table, jostling his coffee cup. "Shit," he growled as the cup fell to the floor, shattering and sending coffee spilling onto the pant leg of the patrons at the next table.

And just like that, all eyes were on him.

Including hers.

He'd been watching her for weeks and he'd seen photos, of course, but he was close enough now to see into her eyes clearly. They were so light brown they were almost golden, highlighted with a coppery ring of gold. She was mesmerizing.

Konner somehow managed to extract himself from the table and step through the mess he'd made, tossing an apology over his shoulder as he moved toward *her*. There was no way he could be so close and not go to her.

She stood impossibly still in the crowd, and vaguely Konner recognized the other patrons and employees had jumped into action to clean up his mess, but he couldn't look away.

Heat flared in his chest, pulling him toward her.

"Do I know you?" Her voice was cool, but there was a hint of warmth underlying her question. She sounded different than she did on her social media channels. *Fuchsia* she was called. An odd choice for a woman so warm, so golden.

"No." Konner forced himself to shake his head a little. "I don't think we've ever met. But we should have." He held her gaze and extended his hand. "I'm Konner." It was only after he'd introduced himself that he thought about using a fake name, but somehow the details of who he was and what he was there to do didn't matter. The only thing that mattered was her.

She looked at his hand, and for a moment, he was afraid she wouldn't take it. Konner was sure he wouldn't be able to be held responsible for what he would do if she didn't. Even if it involved throwing her over his shoulder and carrying her out of the café. Fortunately, she slid her cool, petite hand into his.

The second her skin touched his, the world around him exploded into a frenzy of color, blocking out everything and everyone that wasn't *her*.

Konner had no idea how long they stood that way, her hand in his, their eyes locked on each other, but as far as he was concerned, it wasn't long enough.

"Dakota?"

Dakota.

The name permeated Konner's consciousness, reminding him of why exactly he was there in the first place. He shoved those thoughts out of his mind.

"Dakota?" her friend said again. This time she nudged her, and, to his dismay, Dakota pulled her hand out of his.

He tucked his into his pocket before he did something stupid, like reaching for her in the middle of the crowded coffee shop. Not that his bear thought such a move would be stupid. As far as his animal was concerned, that was the only acceptable thing *to* do.

"Dakota, is it?" Konner forced himself to use her alias. Of course, he knew that already. It was written in his file on the laptop he'd left on the other side of the shop, along with all the other details he'd learned about her. But none of what he'd learned or seen from a distance had prepared him for this moment.

She shook her head a little, her hair shimmering over her shoulder as she seemed to clear her thoughts. "Yes," she said, finally. "I'm Dakota."

"It's nice to meet you, Dakota."

He realized he was staring dumbly at her, but he couldn't bring himself to move. Or blink. Or do anything, really.

"And I'm Ivy." Her friend pushed her way between them

and stuck out her hand. "But I have a feeling you're not going to remember that." She laughed a deep, throaty sound and shook her head before turning to the counter to order.

Konner had a flash of guilt for ignoring the other woman, but the moment Dakota blinked and her golden eyes flashed in his direction once more, it was forgotten. "Sit," he told her. "I'll get you a…" He cleared his throat and tried again. "My table is right over there…" *Shit.* He was screwing this up. He couldn't just tell her what to do. Nor could he expect her to drop everything and join him for a coffee when they'd only just met.

Why not?

They were connected. Mates. He'd known it before, but now…there was no denying it.

A simple coffee didn't seem all that unreasonable when what he really wanted to do was pick her up over his shoulder and carry her out to the woods, where he would tear her clothes off and kiss every inch of her long, lean body before—

"I don't think so."

Her words snapped him back to the moment.

"Excuse me?"

"No." She shook her head and took a step back. "I actually have to…"

She didn't bother to finish the excuse before turning and fleeing the coffee shop, leaving Konner staring after her, fighting against his bear to keep from charging after her.

Chapter Three

NO. *No. No.*

Oh, *hell* no.

Somehow, Dakota managed to pull herself away from the strange man—a *bear*, no less—and get out into the fresh air of the street, away from the overwhelming scent of him that, to her horror, could only be described as intoxicating.

He smelled like vanilla and…was that *seawater*? Like the breeze off the ocean. Like *home.*

No. Not home.

Predator Peak was home now. She'd started over. New town, new life, new *her.*

She needed to protect that life over anything else. Even the pull of a strong, sexy male with eyes that— *No.* Especially from that.

She'd never felt anything like what had just happened between her and the bear. Konner. He said his name was Konner.

Konner.

The air in the coffee shop felt different when she set foot inside. And then there was the smell. But when she'd turned and locked eyes with his, blue like the depths of the very ocean he smelled like, there'd been a pull. A physical tug in her chest that she couldn't control. It was almost painful with its intensity. And when they'd touched…Dakota groaned with the memory. Her skin still felt as if it were on fire.

The sensations were completely new to her but that didn't mean she didn't know what it was.

Dammit.

She needed to get control of herself, because this could not be happening.

Dakota dropped her head and took a deep breath. She flipped her hair back over her shoulder and exhaled slowly.

She was strong. She was in control. She could handle this.

"Dakota!"

Ivy's voice permeated the white noise that was clouding her brain, and she belatedly realized that she still stood in the middle of the street outside Snowdrift. She should have run and gotten as far away from *him* as she possibly could. *Why hadn't he come after her? If he was what she thought he was, he should have come after her, right?*

She spun in a circle, frantically searching. *For Konner? Or a place to hide?* Her brain and the animal inside her were at war.

"Wow." Ivy put a hand on her shoulder. The warm touch steadied her. "That was kind of crazy." Her voice held a humorous lilt. "Just when you think the magic won't—" Ivy's words died on her lips when she saw the look on Dakota's face. "Hey," she said, softer this time. Her voice was full of concern. "What's wrong? Why did you run out of there? I've never seen it happen in front of me before, but that was pretty incredible. And damn, your—"

"Don't say it." Dakota held up a hand. It shook, and she tucked it away. "Please. Don't say it."

"That he's your mate? Or that your mate is sexy as hell?"

Mate.

The word slammed through her, rocking her foundation. Paradoxically, at the same time, the mention of the word settled the cougar inside her, who started to purr.

"I asked you not to say it."

"I don't get it." Ivy shook her head and glanced behind her at the coffee shop, where *he* was still inside. "When it happened to me, you were pretty excited about it. In fact, I seem to remember you making some very inappropriate—"

"Come on." Dakota grabbed her friend's arm and pulled her down the street in the direction of the Well, the bar Ivy's brother Jager owned. "I think I'm going to need something a whole lot stronger than a latte today."

Ivy groaned. She already spent so much time at the bar working or helping out her brother with his little girl, Ruby, so it was usually the last place she wanted to hang out. But just as Dakota knew she would, her friend let herself be led down the street.

Once in the bar and away from *him*—from her *mate*—Dakota still wasn't any closer to being settled. In fact, it was worse. Her cougar was agitated, fighting with her to return to the coffee shop and find him.

But there was no way she could do that. No matter what her instincts screamed at her to do. If she went to him, if she let herself do what every single cell in her body was burning to do...she'd lose everything.

It had been just over a year since she'd left Vancouver. No, since she'd *fled* Vancouver. Dakota had been working on a plan in the back of her mind for years, but when her father announced that she'd be marrying Dominic, a panther shifter from South Florida and the heir apparent to the most brutal and notorious mob family in North America, she'd panicked. She'd only met Dominic a handful of times, mostly when they were teenagers. It was only after their engagement was announced that Dakota realized Dominic had known for years that she was promised to him. It was then that the leering way he'd look at her when he came to town, and his derogatory comments that became more and more sexualized and inappropriate and *graphic*, made sense. His reputation for being a cold, ruthless sadist was well known.

Despite all of that, and knowing exactly what kind of man Dominic was, her father had offered her up like a pig to the slaughter to a horrible man who would undoubtedly commit horrible atrocities toward her. There was no way she could stay and let him claim her.

A shiver racked her body at the thought.

"Here." Ivy pressed her to sit on a barstool. She gestured to Jager and a moment later, a shot of whiskey was put in front of her.

"What's going on?"

Before Dakota could think of anything to say, Ivy answered for her. "She just met her mate. It's fated."

Her best friend's words reverberated in her skull, and she reached for the shot.

"Seems like a reason to celebrate, if you ask me. Where is he?"

"Not here." Dakota glared at Jager. But there was no way to tell her friends that under normal circumstances, finding your mate would be a reason to celebrate—only her circumstances were far from normal.

She downed the shot, letting the whiskey leave a trail of heat down her throat. She gave Jager a quick nod, and he refilled it without question.

"It's not happening."

Ivy let out a laugh and immediately clamped a hand over her mouth. "Come on, Dakota. You saw how well that worked out for me."

It was true. When Ivy met her mate, Nolan, she'd fought it. They both had. Of course, their resistance only drove them both crazy until finally they mated, and now they were living happily ever after. But that was different. For one thing, they were both wolf shifters.

Dakota was a cat.

She was a fucking mountain lion.

Yes, cats mated. But many didn't. They lived solitary lives and were perfectly content. And that was the life Dakota had chosen for herself. When she fled and changed her identity, she'd chosen to be alone forever because it was the only way she could stay safe. Sure, she was lonely sometimes, but it passed. She was fine. Her life was fine. She was doing *fine*. Better than fine because she was safe.

But if she let herself turn toward *him*, if she let him in, if she mated him...nothing would ever be fine again. Because there was no way she could hide from the truth and from the life she left behind to her one true partner. It was known that there was no connection in the world like the one between fated mates. There could be no secrets.

Dakota looked at Ivy, round with her first child. She'd never seen a connection like the one between Ivy and Nolan before. They were fated mates, and it was clear to anyone that Nolan would do anything to protect her.

Would Konner protect her?

Would she be able to trust him?

She didn't even *know* him.

She rolled the shot glass between her hands. *Maybe she could.* But maybe he'd turn on her, too. Money could make people do all kinds of things you would never expect. Would *he* have a price?

She lifted the glass to her mouth and inhaled the sharp, musky liquid before tipping it down her throat.

Dakota had no way of knowing.

And that scared the hell out of her.

Konner didn't have another choice. He had to let her go.

At least that's what he was telling himself to keep from running through the streets, scooping her up and carrying her back to the little house he was renting two streets over. And he couldn't do that. Not because that wasn't what every single part of him wanted to do, what his instincts were screaming at him to do, and what his bear was ready to rip out of his skin for. But because Konner knew if he did, he'd ruin everything. She'd run for a reason. And he knew exactly what it was. Even if she didn't know he knew.

Fuck.

His brain battled with his heart and his base instincts to follow her out to the street. Konner didn't care if everyone was watching as he clenched his fists and worked to control his breathing. She was right there. He could still see her on the street as she struggled for her own breath. She paced back and forth, dropped her head, shook her hair, and finally, when her friend joined her, walked away from him in the opposite direction.

It was only after she was out of eyesight that Konner's bear stopped growling. He gave himself another minute before moving back to his table to collect his things and get the hell out of there. Konner forced himself to turn away and head down the street, away from her.

Dakota.

The name wasn't a surprise. Still, hearing it out loud was different. He liked it. The name suited her a hell of a lot better than her social media name, *Fuchsia.* And much better than her real name, Angelica.

"Shit. Shit. Shit."

Her *real* name. He needed to remember who she really was. Because the captivating woman with the golden eyes he'd just fallen into was *not* Dakota. She was Angelica King, daughter of his boss, who also happened to be one of the most ruthless men in North America. And he'd been hired to do a job. The only thing he was going to do with Angelica, or Dakota or whatever her name was, was take her back to her father, fulfill his debt to him, and move on with his life. He was definitely not going to turn around and track her through the streets so he could declare his undying love for her.

His *mate*? That was ridiculous for so many reasons.

Not the least of all was that he didn't even know her.

You do know her.

His bear was once more alert and unhappy. The farther Konner moved in the opposite direction from Dakota, the more agitated his animal became.

Mine.

Konner growled and clenched his teeth. *No.* She was not *his.* She was a job. A spoiled rotten, entitled princess who'd run off from her cushy life for attention. His job was to bring her back. And that's exactly what he was going to do. And that was *all* he was going to do.

He reached the front door of the small house he'd been renting for the last few weeks. He unlocked the door, slammed it shut behind him, and leaned against the hardwood. He squeezed his eyes shut and worked to regulate his breath. His heart beat too fast, and his breathing refused to slow. He felt the familiar burning in his skin that meant only one thing. He needed to shift. He needed to let his bear out so he could run off this energy. There was no way he'd be able to focus on anything until he did.

Growing up in the city, Konner wasn't used to having the ability to shift whenever he wanted to. Over the years, he'd learned how to control the animal inside him and mostly ignore him. There'd only been a handful of times, mostly when he was a horny teenager trying to figure things out, when he'd felt the overwhelming pull to release his bear and run. But all those times combined didn't come close to the way he was burning with need at that moment.

He dumped his things on the couch, and without pausing, headed straight out the back door. The woods were just beyond the yard. It was hardly unusual to see wild animals running in the woods just on the outskirts of town at any time of day, but the residents tried to be subtle about it, restricting their shifting to the forest. Still, there was a certain amount of freedom, and Konner wasn't used to having the ability to release his animal in mere moments. It was a freedom he was very glad of as he left his clothing in a pile next to a huge spruce and allowed his animal to take over.

His bear was a massive black bear with shiny, thick fur and huge paws. He exploded in a burst of muscle and strength and crashed through the trees at full speed. Since he'd moved to Predator Peak, Konner had explored the surrounding woods a few times, but not enough to know where he was going. And he didn't care.

The only thing he cared about was getting as far away from *her* as he could. Maybe if he ran long and hard enough, he'd be able to forget how his heart had squeezed, his breath caught, and every cell in his body had lit up the moment he'd touched her.

Maybe he'd be able to forget that as much as he wanted her—*needed* her—he'd never be able to have her. Not without losing everything else.

Chapter Four

DAKOTA HAD LOST track of how long she'd been scrolling blindly through social media. It was true that she made her living by posting and engaging with her followers, but she seldom gave in to the time suck temptation of actually using the apps. But since sitting down, she'd watched at least four videos of people getting hurt in sporting activities, three kitten videos, a countless number of cooking tutorials—she didn't even like to cook—and a handful of clips of women pranking their partners.

She'd only picked up her phone in an effort to be distracted. Maybe if she lost herself in other people's lives, even if they were totally fabricated, she'd be able to forget about her own mess of a life for a few minutes.

It hadn't worked. She couldn't stop thinking about Konner.

She threw her phone down on the couch next to her and dropped her head in her hands. She tugged at her hair and let out a low moan that started deep in her chest.

It had been almost a full day since Nolan and Jager had brought her home from the Well, where she'd managed to drink enough whiskey to put her into a deep sleep once she'd been deposited on her couch. But since waking, mercifully without a hangover, *he* once more occupied all her thoughts.

There were a million things she needed to do. She had at least three videos that needed to be posted to her account, never mind the growing number of comments that required responses. Fuchsia had a reputation for being very engaged with her followers. People liked it, and she liked to give them what she wanted. Especially because it resulted in more views, which translated beautifully to more sponsorship deals and higher ad revenue.

Not that she cared about money. She really didn't. If it was a life of affluence and privilege she'd wanted, she never would have left her father and the future he had planned for her. But there was more to life than living that way. Especially if the trade-off was marrying a cruel, sadistic man who'd made it very clear that she would become his property to do with as he liked. Dakota didn't even need to use her imagination to know what he meant by that. On more than one occasion, Dominic had made it very clear exactly how their married life would look, and it was terrifying enough that she'd risked her life to run. She'd rather die on her own terms than hand her life over to him.

As far as Dakota was concerned, money was about survival. She only needed and wanted enough money to stay safe and stay hidden. Which was exactly why she should be working on nurturing Fuchsia's brand instead of lying around, moping about a man she didn't even know.

Mate.

Not a *man*. A *mate*.

Dakota ignored her animal and shook her hair out before arching her back and taking a deep breath. She'd never been the type of woman to moan over a man. Growing up, the few friends she'd had when she was in grade school were constantly infatuated with boys. They'd giggle and whisper about them, draw hearts with their initials and write out their names together, but Dakota had never been able to relate to it. Maybe it was because her father insisted on sending her to a private school where she was the only shifter. Not that it mattered for long. As soon as the boys started to pay even the slightest bit of attention, neither her *friends* nor her father liked it, and Dakota had been pulled from the school system to be privately tutored.

Even so, it wasn't as if she hadn't been exposed to boys or young men at all when she was younger. Despite his best efforts, her father hadn't been able to watch her every minute, and there were plenty of visitors to the house in Vancouver who brought their sons with them. Just because she'd led a controlled and sheltered life didn't mean she wasn't interested in men or curious about her own sexuality. Her father would have been furious if he'd had any idea, but that was part of the thrill. Probably more so than the hookups.

Still, despite having a handful of partners in her life, not once had she felt as if her body was on fire with a simple touch, let alone a look. Not one time had the urge to throw herself into the arms of a man ever taken hold of her so quickly or completely that it was almost as if she had no choice in the matter. The fact that Dakota had been able to muster the strength and sheer will to walk away from him was still something she couldn't comprehend. Because even now, despite all her attempts at distraction, the only thing her brain could focus on for more than five seconds was running down the street until her senses once more filled with the scent of vanilla and seawater so she could claim *him*.

Her mate.

She could try to deny it, but there was no point. She knew it the way she innately knew how to breathe. He was hers and she was his, and she couldn't see any way around it. And that meant she was going to have to figure out a way to—

"I know you're in there."

Dakota jumped at the banging, accompanied by the sound of her best friend's voice outside her front door.

"Let me in, Dakota." The banging got louder. "I have to pee!"

She couldn't help but laugh as she slipped from the couch to unlock the dead bolt.

The moment she did, Ivy burst through the door and headed straight through the living room to the bathroom. "I'll be right back," Ivy called behind her. "I swear, this baby is going to—ahh."

"You could shut the door." Dakota bit back a laugh. After all, she had no idea what it was like to be carrying what had to be a giant wolf-shifter baby in her last trimester of pregnancy. She really did feel for her friend. Every time Dakota saw her, she only seemed to get bigger. It was crazy that she hadn't burst open completely.

"No time," Ivy called. "Besides, this way you can hear what I have to say."

"I can wait." Dakota rolled her eyes. There was nothing Ivy could say to her that would help her situation. Especially considering she didn't know the truth about her either. It's not that she hadn't wanted to tell her best friend who she was and why she was in Predator Peak; she had. Many times. But it was too risky. Especially now. There'd been more messages in her inbox from someone claiming to know who she was, and one, that was scarier, who insisted upon meeting her. That wasn't happening.

Had Konner sent the messages?

There was too much going on, and the inability to think straight was driving her crazy. She needed to go to him. She needed to see him. To touch him. She needed—

"This can't wait."

Ivy started talking loudly from the bathroom, but Dakota had no interest in holding any kind of conversation with someone using the toilet. She rolled her eyes and walked into the kitchen to make tea. A few minutes later, Ivy joined her.

"Did you hear anything I said?"

Dakota shook her head. "You know I didn't." She handed her friend a mug of peppermint tea. "Sit. You look like you're about to fall over."

Ivy gratefully took the mug and sank into a seat. "I feel like it, too. I swear, this baby needs to come already. The midwife was so sure she'd be early, but I'm beginning to think Nolan's going to be right."

"You still have a bit of time before your due date."

"Too long." Ivy groaned dramatically, dropping her head back before grinning. "But I'm not here to complain."

"Could have fooled me."

Ivy raised an eyebrow and gave her a look. "I've come to see how you're holding up."

"Holding up?" Dakota padded across the kitchen to the window over the sink. The blinds were closed, but even so, she was sure someone was out there in the trees, just beyond the yard. *Was she just being paranoid? Or maybe he was watching her. Could that be it? Had it been him all along?* Surely she would have sensed it if her *mate* had been the one following her all this time. "Do you think he'd seen me before?" She spun around, changing the subject. "The bear. Do you think he's been the one watching me?"

"You mean Konner."

Konner. His name vibrated through her body, giving her pins and needles.

"I thought you weren't worried about anyone watching you anymore?"

Ivy narrowed her eyes, but Dakota only shrugged. It was just a little white lie, and only because Ivy had enough to worry about with the baby coming. She didn't need to be worried about Dakota, too. But judging by the look on her friend's face, she wasn't impressed by the move.

"It wasn't a big deal." Dakota waved it away. "But now… well, I…" She turned back to the curtained window. "I think it might have been him. But that would mean he's seen me before. And if that's true, then how come we…"

"Reacted like you'd both been hit over the head by two giant magnets that then pulled you together? You mean, that?" Ivy chuckled. "Maybe it was because it was the first time you'd seen him?" She shrugged. "You know I'm not an expert or anything, and I really have no idea how it works with bears *or* cats. Let alone together."

"Do you think that's weird?" Dakota dropped into the chair across from Ivy, surprising herself with the question. What she should really be asking was how to break the bond or run far away from it. Instead, she felt like a high school girl swooning over a crush. "I mean…a *bear?*"

"You do know that Nolan's brother is mated to a grizzly, right?"

Of course she knew.

"And this town is full of all sorts of combinations," Ivy continued. "So, no. I don't think anything is weird. Especially when it comes to fate. In fact, the one thing I do know for sure is that you can't fight it, Dakota. As much as you seem to want to."

She groaned and dropped her head on the table.

"And I really don't understand *why* you want to fight it." Ivy's voice was laced with confusion. "I mean, you saw first-hand how it made me insane and ultimately, Nolan and I ended up together anyway. It's *fate*, Dakota. You *can't* fight it. Why are you even trying?"

"Because, I…"

Dakota was sick of the secrets. Maybe it was a bad idea,

but given the circumstances, there didn't seem to be a whole lot of *good* choices, so she took a breath and took a chance.

"I've never told you who I am," she started. "Or where I came from."

Ivy held up a hand and shook her head. "And you don't have to, Dakota. You're my friend, and I love you. Your past doesn't matter."

Her friend's words gave her strength. "I really appreciate that."

"I mean it."

"I know you do." She nodded once. "The thing is, there's a reason I never told anyone, and with *him*..." She couldn't bring herself to say his name. "What if—"

"Dakota." Ivy sat up straight in her chair and reached for her hand. "We can sit here and go through every single *what-if*, if that's what you really want to do. But I think there's one thing we can't ignore." She squeezed Dakota's hand in hers. "You're fated. I saw it with my own eyes. And no matter how hard you think about it or fight it, that's the reality. Do you understand what that means?"

Dakota took a deep breath and exhaled slowly. "I think so," she said after a moment.

Unlike her best friend who'd been stubborn enough to attempt to fight fate, Dakota knew better. And she was sharp, always thinking a few steps ahead. That's the only reason she'd managed to stay hidden for so long. And it was exactly what was going to keep her hidden.

Dakota's lips curled up in a sly smile. "If I can't fight fate, then I'm just going to have to control it."

Ivy rolled her eyes, but Dakota didn't care. It was the best idea she'd had. And the only one.

It was going to have to work.

Konner had run his bear well into the night, until he'd been exhausted enough to fall into a restless sleep. As soon as he'd woken in the early morning hours, he'd returned to the woods and once more used his body to the max until he shouldn't have been able to run any longer. And when he'd been certain he would drop, he ran even farther. He pushed himself for hundreds of grueling kilometers, up steep mountains, across rivers and the roughest terrain he'd ever encountered, and still, he couldn't get her out of his mind.

With no other choice, Konner returned to the tree where he'd left his clothes. The burning pull in his chest eased when he drew closer to Predator Peak, where Dakota was, but it still throbbed like a wound. It was as if he had an empty hole inside him that yearned to be filled.

He'd done his best to clear his mind, but even so, the only thought that continued without abatement was of her. Her long, lean legs. Her lightly tanned skin that seemed to sparkle golden in the sunlight. Her long hair that draped perfectly over her slim, slight shoulders and the soft, round mounds of her breasts.

Inside, he turned the tap to the shower and stepped in before the water had a chance to run hot. His cock was thick and hard between his legs. He'd been in an almost constant state of arousal from the moment he'd touched her. He'd been watching her for weeks, and even once or twice he'd come close enough to scent her, but it wasn't until she was right there in front of him that something changed. And when her skin touched his...*fuck.*

Everything changed.

A low moan slipped from his throat as he wrapped his hand around his shaft and let the now lukewarm water stream over him. He stroked himself slowly, her image filling his mind.

He had to have her.

Konner tightened the grip on his shaft and pumped harder.

He leaned forward, letting his free hand hold himself up against the slick tile wall as his right hand worked his pulsing cock.

"Dakota." Her name slipped out with a groan as his balls tightened. He was close, but it wasn't going to be enough. It was never going to be enough until he had his mate beneath him, claiming her for his own.

The image of Dakota naked and wet with desire as he drove his cock into her, pushing her to the ultimate climax at the very moment he sank his teeth in her delicate skin and claimed her as his own was the image in Konner's head as he took his own release under the now steaming hot water of the shower.

He cried out and milked himself before the image of his perfect, beautiful mate faded from his vision.

"Dakota." His voice was little more than a whisper as he pressed both hands against the shower wall and dropped his head. "Mine."

Fuck.

Konner stared at the phone in his hand. He'd already scrolled through half a dozen unread texts and played the three voice messages. The first was from his mother, wondering when he'd be home from his business trip. She knew that Konner worked for Javier King, but she'd never asked for details, and he'd done his best to protect her from them. He hadn't told her he'd gone out of town because he knew she would only worry more than she already did. It was bad enough for her to know her only son was working for the man who was responsible for the death of her husband. Even if she did understand why.

The last two messages were from Sam Ray, King's second-in-command, a stocky, meathead bobcat shifter, who King kept around to do his dirty work. As far as Konner could tell, the only redeeming quality Sam had was that he did what he was told. He was good at following orders and delivering messages. The message he was delivering through voicemail was that the boss was growing impatient with Konner's lack of progress.

Konner had no doubt he'd be delivering a very different, much more physical, message if he didn't finish the job soon. King wasn't the type of man who put up with delays, and Konner was running out of excuses.

He needed to call in an update.

An update he didn't have.

He dialed the number and let his finger hover over the button to connect the call. But he couldn't push it.

"Fuck." He deleted the number and instead pushed the button to call his mother, who answered on the first ring.

"Konner."

The happiness in her voice hit him deep in the chest.

"How are you, honey? You haven't been by. I was starting to get worried."

Guilt flashed through him. With everything his mother had been through because of the King family, he knew better than to cause her any kind of worry at all. "Please don't worry, Mom."

"You know that's impossible." There was a trace of a smile in her voice. "But I trust that you'll make good decisions."

"You know I will, Mom." He was pretty sure there was nothing good about any of the decisions he had to make. Still, there was no point worrying her. Tess Stark had endured more than her share of worry at the expense of his father. "How have you been? How's your wrist doing? Have you been able to work at all?"

The change of subject was easy as Tess filled him in on the latest with the arthritis in her right wrist. She hadn't experienced a flare-up lately and had been able to take on a few new seamstress clients since he'd been gone. His mother worked hard with her sewing machine and was a whiz when it came to altering wedding gowns and other fancy dresses.

"It's prom season," she continued. "Just today, I saw three young women with their beautiful gowns. It would have been so nice to see your sister in a gown for her graduation." He could hear the wistfulness in her voice. "She would have been so pretty in a jade-green dress with her hair down around her shoulders. Simple. Nothing too fancy or frilly. Elegant, just like her."

Konner couldn't help but stifle a chuckle. "I don't know if *elegant* is the word I think of when I think of Cressa."

"Stop it. She's your little sister."

"That doesn't mean I think she's elegant." Konner rolled his eyes. When he thought of his little sister, elegant, dainty, or even feminine weren't the words that came to mind. Bold, stubborn, and badass? Definitely. But whatever version of her little girl his mother saw, Konner just didn't see it. "Besides, Mom, Cressa graduated almost four years ago. I think it's safe to say, it's not going to happen."

"It doesn't mean that I can't dream of it."

He stifled a chuckle.

"Maybe I should start dreaming of a wedding dress?"

Konner almost choked on air. "Is Cressa even dating?"

"You know she isn't. But there's always—"

"I'm not dating either, Mom." He swallowed hard as the pain in his chest flared up. There was no way Konner was going to tell his mother about Dakota. Especially considering there was nothing to tell. It's not as if he could tell her that it appeared he was mated to the King family princess. The very same woman he'd been hired to fetch home in order to pay off his family's debt and free them all forever. Fuck, no. There was *no* way he could tell his mother that. Fate or not.

"You work too hard, Konner." His mother's voice was full of concern. "I know you think you need to—"

"It's not what I think I need to do, Mom. It's what I *have* to do. And speaking of what I have to do, I need to get back to work."

There was a long pause on the other end of the line before, finally, Tess exhaled slowly. "Please be careful, Konner. I know you don't want to tell me what you're doing, and you don't need to."

He could picture her shaking her head and closing her eyes.

"I know enough. And I know very well how ruthless Javier King can be. Promise me you'll be careful."

"I promise, Mom." It wasn't the first time he'd made the promise, but this time when he said the words, they hit a little differently. He had to protect his family. They came first. They'd always come first. And they would definitely come before a selfish spoiled princess only looking for attention.

Konner ended the call and immediately dialed King's direct number, skipping his lackey, Sam.

"Stark." The Mafia boss's voice was smooth, strong, and laced with power. "Where is she?"

"That's why I'm calling. I tracked her to a tiny nothing town in the middle of nowhere." The words were sour in his mouth, but he swallowed hard and pressed on, determined to end this. "She was holed up in a little shack of a house, living like a regular townsperson. Changed her name and everything."

"And now?"

"Now?"

"You said, *was.*"

Had he?

The ache in his chest pulsed and his skin itched, as if simply thinking about Dakota had lit a fire in his gut. He walked to the picture window in the living room and stared down the street in the direction of her house.

"Stark? Are you there?"

"I'm here." Konner blinked and refocused on the conversation. He'd been about to tell King that he'd found his daughter. *His mate.*

"You said was," King continued. "Does that mean you lost her again?"

"I did, sir." Konner hated calling him sir, but it was that or boss. He chose the lesser of the two evils. "She must have caught the scent of me and gotten spooked." The lie slipped easily from his lips before he knew what he'd said. "I only had eyes on her for a few days. Long enough to be sure it was her and come up with an extraction plan that wouldn't be cause for alarm, and then she was gone."

"Fuck."

"I am sorry, sir. I don't know how it happened so fast. I was sure I had her this time."

"She's smart," King muttered under his breath. "Too damn smart." And then, as if he realized Konner was still on the line, he raised his voice to ask, "Where was this? Where did you track her to?"

"The Yukon." Again, the lie came easily.

"So she's still in the country."

"For now." A flash of movement at the end of the street caught Konner's attention. *Dakota.* His animal was alert. He needed to get off the phone. "I have reason to believe she may be moving on to Alaska."

"Alaska? But Angelica hates the cold."

The use of her given name startled Konner. He'd already started thinking of her as Dakota. It suited her.

"Why would she go north?" King wondered out loud.

"Probably because that's where you would least expect to look." Konner hoped like hell he was doing a good job lying.

He needed to buy himself some time. The more the better. "You said yourself how smart she was."

"She is smart. Like her mother."

It was the first time Konner had ever heard mention of Dakota's mother. As far as he knew, King had raised her alone with the help of a rotating group of nannies, tutors, and house-keepers.

"Too smart." His voice hardened. "Find her. Now."

Konner swallowed hard and ended the call.

His eyes were locked on the figure at the end of the street. There was no question about who the smooth, long stride belonged to. Even if he hadn't seen her, he would have sensed her. The closer she got to him, the wilder he felt. Both out of control, and paradoxically calm. He couldn't think straight. It was becoming almost impossible to formulate any thought at all. Except one.

The only thing Konner knew with any clarity was *need*.

He needed her. He needed to be with her. To touch her. To kiss her. To be inside her.

To mate her.

Chapter Five

DAKOTA HAD no idea what she was doing. Not really. The only thing she knew for sure was that she needed to control the situation. And that meant she wasn't going to wait around for him to come to her. She was done with other people making decisions for her, because they historically did whatever benefited them without actually taking her into consideration at all. Screw that. She was a grown woman, and she didn't need or want anyone making decisions for her.

Which was why she needed to control this…situation. Whatever it was.

It's too bad she felt anything but in control.

Her insides were a chaotic mess of instincts, desire, excitement, and fear.

Control.

Calm.

Dakota repeated the words in her head like a mantra to keep herself focused as she approached the house. Not that it was working.

And it wasn't just her heart and mind going haywire. Her chest throbbed. The ache that she'd felt since leaving Konner had turned into a pulsing, hot need. Her body, mind, heart, and animal were all at war with one another. It was a sensation, unlike anything Dakota had ever felt before, that drove her forward.

She could do this. She *had* to do this. Ivy was right. There was no way she could deny fate. She'd seen it firsthand between Ivy and Nolan. They were two of the strongest people she knew, and they'd been no match for fate.

So, if she couldn't deny it, she'd do the next best thing.

Control it.

The problem was, she had no idea what that meant. What she *did* know was that it was becoming almost impossible to stay away from him. She couldn't think straight, and her thoughts were all jumbled. That was dangerous. She needed a clear head to think about her next move and how she could protect herself now that there was this…complication.

She was walking right into the dragon's den—or the bear's den, in this case—and that was probably a bad idea. She had no way to know. The only thing she knew with one hundred percent certainty was that she needed to be with him. She'd sort everything out after that.

With a deep breath, Dakota raised her fist to knock on the door. But before she could make contact, the door swung open and there he was.

She drew in a sharp breath and for the first time since she left her own house, everything was clear. She still had no idea what to do now that she was there, or even how she'd found his house in the first place. It must have been instinct that had taken over.

But it didn't matter. Nothing mattered except the fact that she was there, and he stood in front of her.

Dakota took a step forward, reached up, grabbed his face with both hands and kissed him.

His lips touched hers, and electricity shot through her veins. She held him in place and deepened the kiss.

Konner, momentarily surprised, recovered quickly. "I thought you'd never get here." His voice was low and sexy and full of need.

He bent just enough to wrap his massive hands around her waist and lift her. Dakota wound her legs around him, never once taking her mouth off his. She needed his kiss like she needed air to breathe.

This.

This was what she'd needed. His kiss energized her, fueling her in a way she didn't know she'd been craving. She never wanted it to stop.

Konner held her easily as they continued to make out right there on his front step for anyone to see, but neither of them cared. The only thing that mattered to Dakota was that moment and the feelings that flowed through her.

Her cougar purred but still wanted more.

Konner's hands on her ass held her firmly up against him, and she could feel how much more he needed, too. She ground her pelvis against him, and he groaned. "Maybe we should take this inside?"

With her still held easily in his arms as if she weighed nothing, Konner backed up and into the house. He kicked the door shut and pushed her up against the wood. With one hand free, he cupped her cheek and tipped her head back to give him access to her neck. His lips left hers to kiss the sensitive skin below her ear, sending a fresh round of desire racing through her.

Control.

Her brain screamed at her.

Control, Dakota. You have to control this.

With Konner kissing her neck and grinding his impossibly huge and hard cock against her, control was not the word she would use to describe the situation. Her cougar didn't care. The only thing she cared about was the moment at hand and this man. Her mate.

Mate.

She warred with herself and, for a moment, Dakota was sure she was going to lose herself over to her animalistic desires and the pull of fate that was almost too strong to resist.

Control!

Her eyes popped open, the spell of the moment broken. "Wait." The word slipped from her throat, barely louder than a squeak. Konner's mouth was on her collarbone, nipping and kissing and sending all kinds of wild sensations through her, but he stilled when she said his name. "Konner. Wait," she said again.

He lifted his head and looked into her eyes. She was immediately pulled into the bright blue of his irises and almost forgot what she'd been trying to say or why she needed him to stop what he was doing when it felt so fucking good. *Almost.*

Dakota squeezed her eyes shut. "I just need a minute. There's been so much…it's all so… everything…" She couldn't formulate a complete thought. "Can you put me down for a second?"

She hated asking because she knew she was going to miss his touch the moment it was gone.

Konner flinched but didn't hesitate. He lowered her slowly to the ground and took two steps back, giving her space.

Just as Dakota suspected, the second his hands were off her, the only thing she could think of was how she could get them back on her and how fast she could make it happen. She squeezed her hands together to keep her focused and to keep from lunging for him again.

"I'm sorry." Konner scrubbed a hand over his face and shook his head a little. "I shouldn't have done that."

"You didn't do anything." Dakota tipped her head to the

side. "The way I remember it, *I* kissed *you*."

"That's right." His mouth twitched up into a very sexy grin. "You did." He bit his bottom lip, and a groan slipped from Dakota.

She shook her head and forced herself to focus on the situation. "I have a few questions."

It was a monumental understatement.

Konner nodded. "I imagine you do."

"You don't?"

"Oh, I have one or two." He chuckled. "You first."

She blew a breath and wrapped her arms around her chest as a barrier. "Who are you?"

"My name is Konner Stark. I'm a bear shifter."

She already knew that.

"I'm your mate."

His words caused a visceral reaction within her. She tightened her grip on herself. She knew that, too. "Did you know?"

He shook his head once. "Not until you walked into the coffee shop."

"How?"

"Your guess is as good as mine." He shrugged his massive shoulders.

Instantly, Dakota's mind flashed to how easily he'd lifted her and held her up against his hard chest as if she weighed nothing. She squeezed her eyes shut against the image, but they flew open again when he said, "Fate."

"Fuck fate," she mumbled under her breath and ran her hands through her hair.

"Hey. I heard that."

Dakota looked up into Konner's eyes and immediately felt bad for her gut reaction. "That's not what I meant," she said quickly. "I just meant that I'm not really in a place in my life where I want a mate and…why is it so hard to look at you and not want to…"

"Rip your clothes off and kiss every inch of your body until you're screaming my name?"

His words, or maybe the way he looked at her as if he could devour her at any moment, caused a rush of wet heat to pool between her legs. Konner's nostrils flared. *Could he scent her desire?* The idea only turned her on more.

"Yeah." Dakota nodded dumbly. "That."

His lips quirked up into a cocky grin. "I imagine it's that fate thing we were just talking about." He moved to step toward her but stopped himself. "Fuck, Dakota. I don't understand it either, but even from a distance, I knew there was something special about you. But then, when I saw you in the coffee shop, it was as if something inside me split wide open." Again, he visibly held himself back from her. "This pull toward you..." He took a deep breath and exhaled slowly. "I can hardly fight it."

His words hit that spot inside her that had been aching uncontrollably all day, and her animal took over. Before she knew what she was doing, she took a step forward. "Maybe we should just stop fighting."

"That's the best idea I've heard all day."

It wasn't until his mouth was on hers again, his hands all over her body, tearing the clothes from her body, that Dakota registered what he'd said moments before. *Even from a distance.*

Had he been the one watching her? Had he been following her? Was Konner the reason she'd been hiding in her house, scared to walk alone? And if he was, why?

They were all good questions. Vitally important ones, too. But as her hands found the smooth, hard skin beneath his T-shirt and her fingers worked to free Konner's hard cock from his jeans, none of the details mattered. Nothing mattered but having this man naked and inside her.

And as for *control*...fuck control.

Passion ignited his thoughts, leaving no room for reason. All the blood had rushed from his brain and the animal inside him was firmly in control. His bear roared as he tore Dakota's clothing from her body. She was even more beautiful naked. Her skin glowed in the late afternoon sunlight that streamed through his living room windows. For a moment, Konner contemplated taking her upstairs to the bedroom, but there was no time. His bear would not be satisfied until he had her. And then maybe he'd be able to think straight. At least long enough to figure out what the fuck he was going to do about her.

But that would have to wait. Because there was only one thing he wanted to think about at the moment.

His mate.

He trailed one hand up her side, forcing himself to slow down and enjoy every part of her long, lean body. But when Dakota pulled down the zipper of his jeans and her hand wrapped around his thick cock, it was almost his undoing.

Konner groaned and used one hand to brace himself against the door as the sensation of her delicate touch threatened to drop him to his knees.

"Fuck, woman. Are you trying to kill me?"

"Oh no," she purred. "You wouldn't be any good to me then." Her tongue darted out and licked her bottom lip before she sucked it between her teeth.

A man could only handle so much. A growl ripped from his chest. He closed the distance between them, grabbing both her hands as he did. He pinned her arms above her head against the wall as he pushed her back with enough force to make her squeal a little. Konner forced himself to pause long enough to check in with her. Her eyes were heavy with desire, her breath coming fast, causing her breasts, now perfectly on display for him, to heave with every quick breath she took.

He held both her wrists easily in one hand and trailed the other down between her breasts, past her belly button, to the cleft between her legs. The scent of her desire, sweet and spicy, had hung heavy on the air between them since she'd walked in, but now it was overwhelming his senses and driving out thoughts of anything else but having her. His mate.

"Dammit, kitten." The pet name came easily, a perfect fit for his wild cat. He shook his head and sucked in a sharp breath in an effort to control himself. "I don't know...I need to...I'm going..." He growled and tore his gaze from hers.

"Stop talking, *bear*."

Konner looked back to see her thrusting her tits up and arching her back. She wriggled with need, but Konner's grip held her fast.

"You want this?" It seemed like an obviously redundant question, but given the completely insane situation they found themselves in, it seemed appropriate.

Her eyes narrowed and her tongue darted out between her lips. "I *need* this. Now."

He didn't have to be told twice.

Konner dropped her arms long enough to shed himself from the rest of his clothes. Seconds later, he had her pinned up against the wall again. He scooped her up easily and lifted her, so she only just hovered over his cock. It was only then that he remembered a condom. *Fuck.*

He moved to put her down, but she stopped him. "I'm on birth control."

It was all he needed to hear. Konner began to slowly lower her onto his throbbing, hard cock. She cried out and he paused, giving her a moment to adjust to him. Her snug, wet heat felt amazing, and it was an exercise in control to keep from plunging deep. But he'd wait. Fortunately for him, mere seconds later, she thrust her hips up to meet him, seeking more of him. He gave it all to her and when he was fully seated inside her, she dropped her head back and groaned.

Shock waves of pleasure slammed into him as he started to move. Dakota felt unlike anything he'd ever experienced before. He braced one hand against the wall for leverage and began to move in earnest. Her legs wrapped tightly around his waist and squeezed with every thrust. They moved in perfect unison, both quickly moving toward release.

Dakota lifted her head. Her golden eyes flashed, and her lips parted. It was the sexiest thing he'd ever seen and was almost his complete undoing. But then she leaned forward and took his mouth with hers, kissing him.

Konner knew he wasn't going to last much longer. And when he felt her clench and tense around his cock, he knew they were going to lose it together. He held off until finally he felt her begin to quiver. She pulled her mouth from his and pressed her face against his chest. Her climax ripped through her, and she cried out as Konner lost control himself. He threw his head back, and his bear roared out as the orgasm began to rip through him.

A hot, sharp heat pricked at his chest. Somehow, in the haze of his desire, Konner focused on Dakota, whose mouth was pressed to his chest. Instantly, he knew what she was doing: sealing their bond. His bear roared with pleasure as Konner took his final release into her wet heat.

It was only after the haze cleared, and Konner looked down at Dakota, still held firmly in his arms up against the wall, that he realized she'd never completed the bite to seal the bond. Instead, her cheek was pressed up against his chest. Her eyes were closed, and a single tear glistened on her dewy skin.

His heart squeezed in his chest.

Dakota was his fated mate—of that, he was absolutely certain. But, sometimes maybe not even fate was enough.

Chapter Six

DAKOTA EXAMINED herself in the mirror.

She looked exactly the same.

How was that even possible, when she felt so incredibly different?

It's not as if she hadn't had sex before. Of course she had. But that…with Konner…*that* hadn't been sex.

That had been something very, very different.

Holy hell. She'd almost bit him.

The memory of her teeth piercing his smooth, deliciously salty skin before she was able to pull away, mere seconds before she'd done something she could never take back, flooded through her, and she had to look away from her reflection.

Not biting him had been the hardest thing she'd ever done. But it had been the only thing she *could* do. She couldn't take a mate right now. It didn't make sense. It wasn't safe. Let alone the fact that she didn't even know who he was. How could she seal the mate bond with a *stranger?*

But he wasn't a stranger. Not in any of the ways that mattered. Dakota knew none of her arguments were valid any longer. Now that she'd had a taste of him, had him inside her, kissing her, pulling incredible pleasure out of her with such ease, there was no way she was going to be able to walk away from him.

Shit.

Once more, she stared at herself in the mirror. Her eyes flashed bright and her pupils dilated. She was so screwed. If she stayed with him, she would risk everything. *What if he found out who she really was? She couldn't keep that from him, could she? And if he did learn the truth, would he turn on her? Or would he protect her?* A mate was supposed to put their partner above all else.

At the same time, she knew she couldn't *not* stay with him.

There was no easy way out.

A knock on the bathroom door jolted Dakota out of her thoughts.

"Dakota?"

Her entire body reacted to her name on Konner's lips. Her cougar mewled. Dakota wanted to cry.

"Are you okay in there?"

"I'll be right out." She tried not to inhale the scent of him while she quickly pulled on the T-shirt and pair of drawstring workout shorts he'd given her to wear considering he'd destroyed the clothes she'd been wearing.

All she'd wanted when she'd arrived at his house was to be in control of the situation and now...*shit.* Things were so far from being in control it was laughable. Being with Konner hadn't made anything clearer. If anything, things had just become a whole lot murkier.

She almost laughed out loud at how naive she'd been less than an hour ago. To think she could wield any level of control over fate was ridiculous. Because the closer she'd gotten to Konner, the wilder her animal got, and then it was too late. She couldn't have turned away even if her life had been at stake. She'd been completely at the mercy of fate. The same way she'd known the second her lips touched his that she wouldn't be walking away from him.

What was she going to do?

Her mind spun.

They'd slept together but she hadn't mated with him, so there was still a chance of—what? Walking away? Her cougar hissed at the idea. *But what was the other choice?*

Mate, her animal screamed at her.

No closer to any answers, Dakota took one last look in the mirror. She looked tiny in his clothes so many sizes too big. She inhaled deeply and exhaled slowly, put a smile on her face, left the bathroom, and joined Konner in the living room.

"Hey. I was beginning to get worried."

Konner moved toward her, but there must have been something in her expression because he stopped and tucked his hands in the front pocket of the jeans he'd put on while she was in the bathroom. He hadn't put his shirt on yet, a small detail Dakota found herself very thankful for as her eyes roamed over his chiseled chest muscles.

Damn. The man was incredible. Her gaze moved to the spot on his smooth skin, right over his heart, where she'd almost let herself go. She swallowed hard and forced herself to look away.

"Sorry." She shook her head. "I just needed to...I had to..." She blew out a breath. "You know what? I think I should just go." Dakota moved quickly past him and reached for the door handle.

"You don't want to leave."

To his credit, Konner didn't try to physically stop her, or block the door. His words were effective enough on their own to stop her in her tracks. With her hand on the doorknob, Dakota slowly turned.

"What makes you so confident?"

"Because if you're feeling even a fraction of what I'm feeling right now, then I know you don't want to go anywhere."

He wasn't wrong, and it pissed her off.

She crossed her arms over her chest and narrowed her eyes, unwilling to give him the satisfaction of being right. "And what exactly are *you* feeling?" Dakota knew she was being a bitch, but she couldn't stop herself.

"I'm feeling whole and complete in a way I've never felt before."

His eyes locked on her with such intensity, it sent a shiver down her spine.

"I feel like my body has woken up in a way that makes me think I've been sleepwalking my entire life. When you're close to me and when I'm touching you, it's like I can finally fill my lungs for the first time in my life."

His words were genuine. And it was exactly how she felt about him.

Konner took a step toward her. "I didn't even know I was missing you, Dakota. I was going through life perfectly fine without you. But now that you're here, I know with one hundred percent certainty that I cannot be without you. If I let you walk out of here, it will be like I'm killing a part of myself." He closed his eyes and dropped his chin to his chest for a moment before continuing. "I know I can't keep you here if you don't want to stay, and I won't ever ask you to do something you don't want to do. But I am going to ask you right now not to lie to yourself. You don't want to leave. I know it like I know I'm standing in front of you right now. Stay."

The air slipped from her lungs as she digested everything he'd said.

Despite his massive size advantage over her, in that moment, he was incredibly vulnerable as he waited for her response. And something inside her shifted.

He was right. She didn't want to leave. Not ever. But she didn't know how to stay.

"It's not a good idea."

"I disagree. It's a very good idea." His lips twitched as he tried not to smile. "Don't tell me that you think what happened between us wasn't a good idea either."

"It—"

"Ah." He held up a finger and wiggled his eyebrows. "I told you not to tell me."

It was so disarming, that despite herself, Dakota laughed. She clamped a hand over her mouth, but it was too late. She dropped her head for a moment and when she looked up, Konner had a goofy smile on his very sexy face.

"I wasn't going to tell you that," she lied, but she couldn't help but smile as she did so. It was so easy to be around him. Dakota didn't think she'd ever experienced such ease with someone before. When she was young, everyone treated her as though she were breakable, like a fragile doll that needed to be *managed*. And since she'd run away, the walls she put up around others were of her own making. Even with Ivy, her closest friend, there was a resistance that made it hard to trust and be totally herself. But with Konner, even in such a ridiculously short time, she didn't feel self-conscious or judged. She just felt…loved.

And that was the most ridiculous thing ever, considering she hardly knew him.

"Is that right?" He took another small step toward her.

She nodded, surprising herself that she hadn't already turned and fled. "That's right." Not only that, she took another small step toward him.

"Then you were probably going to tell me how amazing it was and how it was the best part of your day." His eyes sparkled with mischief, and what was left of her reservations melted away.

"That wouldn't be a lie."

"No," he said, suddenly serious. "It wouldn't."

His pupils dilated and his nostrils flared. The way he

looked at her sent thrills through her body and filled her with an immediate hot need for him. Again.

Konner held his hand out. "Stay."

There was nothing else she could do.

Dakota was currently curled up in the corner of the sofa with her arms wrapped around her long, bare legs. Her hair fell over her shoulder, and she looked straight up delectable in his simple T-shirt and shorts.

"Here." Konner handed her a plushy blanket.

"Um, thanks." She took it with a question in her eyes. "But I'm not cold."

"Maybe not." He shook his head. "But if I'm going to have any hope of having a conversation with you, which I very much want to do, without tearing those clothes off you and kissing my way up your body, you need to cover up."

She grinned and pulled the blanket over her legs, but not before Konner caught the scent of her arousal.

"Thank you." He took the easy chair across from her but moved it closer before he sat down.

He wanted to respect the fact that despite the hot sex up against the door, and the whole *fated mate* thing, they still didn't know each other, and it was probably a good idea to take things slowly at first, at least until they got to know each other a little bit.

She was his mate. It was a detail he still needed to wrap his mind around—his body was already totally on board. He needed to focus on the bond they shared and how to solidify that before he sorted out the details of everything else. One thing at a time.

Konner leaned forward in the chair, needing to be as close to her as possible. There was such a strong connection between them, he felt as though his bear would tear right out of his skin if he wasn't near her. "I don't want to come off like an asshole who thinks it's your job to cover up just so I can control myself. Please know I'm not like that." He shook his head. "Not at all. I have a little sister, and I would never try to tell her it's her fault if a man—"

"Konner." She stopped him with her hand. "It's okay. I understand." Dakota shrugged. "Well, I don't. Not really. But...you know." She adjusted the blanket around her.

Even though he couldn't see her long, smooth legs, he could picture them clearly and remember what they felt like wrapped around his back while he sank himself into her. Despite himself, a growl slipped from his throat.

She sat back and giggled nervously.

"I'm sorry, Dakota." Konner shook his head. "I can control myself. I promise. And I can control my bear, too. I really do want to just..." He longed to reach out to touch her, but he knew despite her laughter, she was still on edge. He sat on his hand. "I want to talk."

"Talk?" She sat up a bit. "Okay." A smile slipped across her face, and this time there was nothing tentative about it. "I like that idea. I mean, we're clearly..." She gestured between them. "Connected."

It was Konner's turn to laugh. "Oh, we're connected all right."

"No denying that."

"Nope." He shook his head. "You should know, I wasn't expecting this." He paused, careful about how much he should reveal to her. This was uncharted territory, because not only had he not expected it, he didn't want it. A fated mate right now was a big enough problem. But the fact that he'd been hired to kidnap his mate and return her to her father and sadistic fiancé was a *massive* problem. And he certainly couldn't tell her about that. If she knew the truth, she'd run. And if that happened, his bear wouldn't be able to handle it. Some things would have to stay a secret for a little longer. At least until he figured out what he was going to do about it.

Everything in his life had been turned upside down in a matter of twenty-four hours because of this woman sitting across from him. But instead of being pissed off about it, all Konner could think about was how to get even closer to her. He desperately wanted to know everything about her. He wanted to touch her. Kiss her. Make love to her. Hell, he just wanted to *be* with her.

Oh yes, thinking about Dakota as a job would have been much easier. He still didn't know much about her, but it was clear by the little he did know that she was nothing like the spoiled, bratty princess he'd expected. The only other thing that was clear was that there was no way he would do anything that would bring harm to her in any way. Konner knew that with perfect clarity. The only thing he hadn't figured out yet was how he was going to accomplish that and pay off his debt.

There would be time for that later. Right now, the only focus was on *her*. "I get the impression you weren't expecting it either."

She laughed, a deep, throaty sound that rolled from her. "Not even a little. You should know that I don't usually do…" She pointed to the door and then to him. "That," she finished lamely.

"You mean you don't usually walk up to a stranger's front door and throw yourself at them?"

She threw a pillow at him.

He caught it easily and winked. "I'm certainly glad you did this time. After the coffee shop…" He sucked in a deep breath. "I couldn't think straight. It was driving me crazy, not being near you."

She nodded and bit her bottom lip. She didn't need to tell

him that she'd felt exactly the same way. After all, she'd come to him.

"But you should know." He took a deep breath, still not sure how much he should reveal. "If you hadn't come to me, I would be knocking down your door right now." Huge understatement.

"Fate, huh?" She shrugged in an apparent offer to come off flippant, but there was nothing casual about what she'd said.

"Yes." Konner's voice was serious, his gaze focused. He needed to make her understand how much she was affecting him. *Did she even know what she was doing to him? Was he having the same effect on her?* "You should know that not touching you right now is an immense test of my self-control." She opened her mouth to speak, but he continued quickly. "I won't," he said. "Not if you don't want me to. Just being next to you is calming my bear. I can't even explain how unsettled I've been since…well…"

"You don't need to explain anything." She exhaled slowly. "I feel the same."

"You do?"

"You know I do."

He did.

She'd been about to bite him earlier, but something had stopped her from claiming him as hers. "Why did you stop?" He had to know. She tilted her head in question, so he did his best to clarify. "You were going to claim me, but something stopped you. What was it?"

Dakota took a breath and exhaled slowly. Konner watched as myriad emotions flashed over her face. "Why didn't *you* bite *me*?"

He was taken aback by the turnaround of the question. "Is that what you wanted?" His voice was gruff. Unable to hold himself back any longer, he reached out and cupped her calf with his hand. Even through the fluffy blanket, he could feel the heat of her. "Are you old-fashioned?" His fingers wrapped around her leg.

"Yes." She breathed the word but seemed to catch herself a moment later. "I mean, no." Dakota shook her head a little, but she didn't pull away from his touch. "Yes, I wanted you to bite me, but I didn't really realize it at the time, and no, I'm not old-fashioned. At least I don't think I am." She squeezed her eyes shut for a moment. "The reason I didn't claim you was because…"

She didn't need to finish the sentence, for Konner to know what she was going to say.

"You didn't plan on staying."

She nodded once.

"You thought you were going to be able to get me out of your system that easily?" He wiggled his eyebrows and shifted closer to her so he could take her other leg in his free hand. The blanket was starting to become a cumbersome annoyance.

"I actually didn't know what I was going to do," she admitted. "But that was my hope, yes."

He wasn't surprised by it, knowing what he knew about her. Still, the idea that she thought she'd be able to walk away from him made him crazy.

"And now?" He let his fingers trail up to her knees. "Do you still think you can walk away from me?"

The sweet scent of caramel and chai gave away her arousal. It was the only answer Konner needed, but he wanted to hear it from her mouth, too.

She swallowed hard, bit her bottom lip, and shook her head a little. "I know I can't."

Chapter Seven

IT WAS THE TRUTH, and they both knew it. Just like they knew he wouldn't be able to walk away from her.

It was fate.

"We're doing this." It wasn't a question. Dakota twined her fingers in Konner's and squeezed. They were doing this. Whatever *this* was.

"I don't know much about fate." His lips twitched up in a smile. "But I don't think we have much of a choice here at all." He finished the thought by pulling her hand to his mouth and pressing a kiss to it.

"No." Dakota took a breath. Something about being with him, when he was touching her, made her forget about all the reasons they shouldn't be together. And there were so many. Like the fact that she couldn't let anyone into her heart. She had secrets, and they were a matter of life or death.

He's your mate.

Not only did she know that, she *felt* it. He was her mate. Her one. Her only. *But did that mean she could trust him with the truth?*

There was no way to know for sure.

She had to trust, because it was the only thing she could do. Leaving wasn't an option. That much she knew with certainty. The connection between them was too strong to ignore. Turning her back on this would be near impossible. And that's what she needed to focus on for now. She'd figure out the details later.

"I didn't play very hard to get earlier, did I?"

"No." Konner pinched his chin and shook his head. "But you don't hear me complaining, do you?"

She tilted her head and eyed him. "You're definitely not complaining."

"But?"

Dakota shrugged, letting her hair fall over one shoulder. She was very aware she was flirting with him, something she had almost no practice with, yet with Konner it came naturally.

"I think I see what you're getting at." His lips quirked up in a sly smile.

"You do, do you?"

"You're looking for a little seduction?"

Dakota had to bite her lip to keep from laughing out loud. He hardly needed to seduce her; that much was already clear. Still, if he wanted to give it a shot… "I wouldn't complain."

He held her gaze as he once more brought her hand to his lips and pressed a kiss there. "Challenge accepted."

Before she could respond, Konner left his seat and moved smoothly next to her on the sofa. The couch cushions sank under his weight. Dakota didn't resist gravity and her body naturally sank toward him; Konner lifted his arm and welcomed her into his embrace.

She fit perfectly in the crook of his arm. Her heart rate slowed, her breathing evened out, and everything felt calm the moment Konner dropped his hand to her shoulder.

She felt at home with him in a way she'd never felt before.

Not in the house she'd grown up in. Not even in the little house she'd bought with cash in Predator Peak. She'd never felt as at ease and as safe as she did in that moment with Konner.

"It will be much easier to seduce you from here."

He trailed his fingers over her arm, sending shivers through her, and Dakota knew she was already gone. She was pretty sure he only needed to be in the room, and she would happily throw herself at him.

"This really isn't much of a challenge, Konner."

"That doesn't mean I'm not going to keep trying." He lowered his head and kissed the top of her head. "You smell...delicious."

"What do I smell like?"

She turned a little in his embrace so she could see his face when he answered.

"Like caramel." He inhaled deeply and lifted her hair from her head, letting the strands slide through. "With a trace of chai. Not at all like I thought you would."

His choice of words triggered an earlier memory when her brain had been foggy with desire and unable to focus. Dakota forced herself to sit up a little further so she could look at him better. "What do you mean, not what you thought I'd smell like? Earlier you said something about the first time you saw me."

"And I couldn't stay away from you." He placed a hand on her upper thigh, letting his finger trace small, casual circles on the bare skin.

Her body yearned to lean into him and press up against him so she could rub every part of her on his body until they were both purring with the pleasure of it.

"Right." Dakota stroked his hand with her own, encouraging his touch. "But before that. You said something about the very first time you saw me."

Even from a distance, I knew there was something special about you.

Her memory started to crystallize. He'd definitely mentioned seeing her before that time in the coffee shop when they'd connected. And the more she let herself think about it, all the pieces fell into place. "It was you," she said. "You were following me." When he didn't deny it immediately, she knew for sure. "Why?"

Her mind spun. It had been him who'd followed her. Who'd terrified her. For weeks, she'd been afraid to open her blinds or even go outside on her own because she could feel his eyes on her. She'd been absolutely terrified because of *him*. Yet, despite all of that, she felt safe with him in this moment. None of it made sense. His hand on her leg reassured her. She should be running away from him, but all she wanted to do was get even closer than she already was.

And that only confused her more.

"Konner." Her breath hitched in her chest, but she needed to know. "Why were you following me?"

He sat back and inhaled deeply. "I need you to hear me out." He tipped his head a little and for a moment, he looked so bashful and vulnerable that she melted a little more into his touch. "When I first got to town, I was only looking for a quiet place to work on my book and get away from life for a while. And then, one day, I caught a glimpse of you. Not up close," he added quickly. "We all know what happened the first time I saw you up close."

She blushed and immediately felt ridiculous. This man brought out all kinds of things in her—including, apparently, the ability to act like a schoolgirl. It was unsettling, but also she kind of liked it.

"Anyway, when I saw you from afar, I felt something, but I couldn't be sure what it was." Konner nodded a little, as if he were remembering the exact moment.

Dakota leaned into the story, eager to know what he felt when he saw her for the first time. She should have been on edge, getting ready to run away from this man who'd just admitted to stalking her for weeks, but her instincts told her she was safe and he wouldn't hurt her.

"Like I said, I wasn't looking to meet anyone. I just wanted to keep a low profile in town to write my book. But my bear couldn't leave you alone, so I tried to keep my distance before I knew exactly what was happening. Does that make sense?"

She shook her head, and Konner laughed. "I guess it probably doesn't really sound believable, but I think I must have known deep down that if I allowed myself to meet you, I'd get…" He let his hand trail up her leg a little bit, which sent shock waves racing through her. "Distracted."

"And you're distracted now?"

"Oh, I think it's safe to say I'm very, very distracted." His nostrils flared. He leaned in and Dakota was sure he was going to kiss her, but he pulled back and looked at her seriously. "I am so sorry if I scared you by following you, Dakota." He moved his hand and cupped her cheek. "It was never my intention to cause you distress or upset you in any way. I hope you believe me."

He hated lying to her. It made him sick inside, but Konner didn't have another choice. Fate had spoken, and there was nothing clearer in his life. She was his. And he was hers.

Losing her was not an option.

And that meant lying.

Her face, still cupped in his hand, was fragile and vulnerable. She looked up at him with trusting eyes. It was only a little white lie. It wouldn't hurt her. The truth *would* hurt her, and he was never going to hurt her. Not ever.

"I'll never hurt you, Dakota." Konner put his free hand on

her other cheek and looked deep into her eyes. "I never expected this, and I know you didn't either."

She blinked slowly but didn't disagree with him.

"But it's happening. It's fate. And I think you know as well as I do that we can't fight it." He swallowed hard. "And even if we could," he continued, "I don't want to." He let his thumb stroke small circles on her cheek. "Because the only thing I want is you. I *need* you."

He kissed her. Slow and sensual at first. Her lips were soft and giving against his.

Dakota pulled away and nestled her face in the crook of his neck. "I need you, too."

His heart clenched in his chest when she added, "And that scares me."

Her vulnerability washed through him. She was opening up, but there was still so much she was holding back. Of course, she didn't know that he knew that, and he couldn't tell her that he knew. All he could do was show her that he meant what he'd said. He would never hurt her.

She was scared and that made total sense. How could she *not* be terrified? He still didn't know why she'd run away from her life, although he was starting to piece together a very different picture than the one King had painted for him. There was nothing about his mate that was spoiled or selfish. Dakota wasn't the vapid, socialite princess only looking for attention that he'd been led to believe she was.

No, his mate was nothing of the sort.

More than anything, Konner wanted her to trust him with the truth. But she was a cat, and mountain lions weren't known to open up and let in others easily. It would come.

Konner lifted her face and kissed her gently. "I've got you, Dakota. No matter what." He pressed kisses to each of her cheeks and then her nose and forehead. Her eyes were closed, and a single tear slipped down her cheek as he moved his kisses lower, to the neckline of the oversized shirt she wore.

Moving slowly, he let his hands travel down her sides to find the hem of the shirt and slip beneath it. He splayed his large hands over her tiny rib cage and let the heat from his touch calm her before he lifted the shirt from her body and covered her belly, ribs, and perfect tits in a hundred soft, gentle kisses.

"Is this part of your seduction?" She tried to joke with him, but her eyes gave her away.

"Kitten, this is so much more than that." He pressed a kiss between her breasts.

She groaned as she arched her back, an invitation for more.

"I vow to protect you and keep you safe." His voice was soft as he pulled one nipple between his lips and sucked gently until a moan slipped from her throat. Konner moved his attention to her other breast, circling the nipple with his tongue before suckling it, too, for a moment.

Dakota squirmed and let her head fall back against the couch.

He stood and shed his jeans before kneeling on the floor in front of the couch. He looked up at his beautiful mate and sucked in a sharp breath. She was absolutely stunning. Everything about her was perfect. And the way she exposed her vulnerability to him, the trust she was putting into his hands, just made her that much more special and concreted his desire to protect her above all else. But first, he needed to make her his. It was becoming all consuming and overwhelming, the need to solidify their bond and mate her properly flowed through his veins like liquid fire.

He reached up and tugged the oversized shorts from her body before trailing kisses up the length of first one leg, and then the other. Dakota groaned and spread her legs for him. The scent of her sweetness flooded his senses, and it was with an overwhelming effort that Konner was able to control himself. He lowered his head between her legs and licked down her seam.

Dakota cried out and her hips jumped off the couch. He held her in place with his massive hands and licked her again. And again, until the sweet taste of her coated his tongue.

His cock, thick and impossibly hard, throbbed between his legs. But he would have to wait. This was about her. And bonding her to him.

Konner focused his attention on Dakota's sweet core, kissing and sucking and letting his tongue swirl through her heat until her entire body vibrated. Her hands tangled in his hair. She tugged, and he increased his efforts.

"Konner." Her voice was hardly more than a breath.

He pulled away from her and looked up to see her head still thrown back. A sheen of sweat glistened over her beautiful breasts that heaved with her quick breaths. "Dakota. Look at me," he commanded.

She complied, her eyes fluttering open as she lifted her head.

"I need you," he said simply. "You are mine, and I am yours."

Her head bobbed in agreement. "I am yours."

"Mate," he growled.

Once more she tried to buck her hips, but he had her pinned. "Konner, I need you…I need…"

"Kitten, I know exactly what you need."

She groaned and dropped her head back again.

Again, Konner kissed her pussy, letting his tongue draw the desire out of her. She was close. Right on the edge of climax. He drew her closer and then pulled back, keeping her release just out of reach.

She tried to press her legs together, but Konner held her still. He flicked his tongue over her bud until finally he could feel the tension in her body begin to coil. It was only then that he released one leg to free his hand and slipped first one finger, then another inside her wet heat.

Dakota cried out as her orgasm started to take over. Konner hooked his fingers and pressed up to the sweet spot inside her as he kissed and licked the soft, sensitive skin on the inside of her thigh.

Her orgasm came on hard, crashing through her in an uncontrollable wave. Konner roared and sank his teeth into her thigh as Dakota lost herself completely to the ecstasy that took over her body.

Mine.

My mate.

Chapter Eight

MATE.

Dakota tilted her head up from where it rested on Konner's chest to look at his face. His features were softer while he slept, but even at rest, his strength and power were evident. She resisted the urge to trace a finger down his cheek to where his lips were slightly parted. He slept deeply, the same way she had once they moved from the couch to the bedroom where he'd mated her.

Her hand moved between her legs to feel the mark Konner had left there. It was still raw, but it didn't hurt. Even when he'd marked her, the only sensation she'd had was pure bliss rocketing through her and the most intense orgasm of her life. Hell, Dakota didn't even know sex could feel like that. She closed her eyes and let her fingers travel between her legs, where she was swollen with the slightest ache from their lovemaking.

A sigh slipped from her lips.

Mate.

The word still felt foreign and a little strange, but it didn't scare her the way she'd expected it to. In fact, it was exactly the opposite. The restless, edginess of constantly looking over her shoulder that she'd been living with since running away from her father was completely gone. The wild spinning in her mind that had taken over after the first time she'd laid eyes on Konner was gone, too.

For the first time in recent memory, maybe ever, Dakota felt at peace.

Logically, she knew she should be freaking out over the fact that Konner, who was a virtual stranger to her, had just claimed her as his mate. She was mated. To a *bear*. But she wasn't freaking out. Not even a little bit.

Dakota snuggled closer to her mate and sighed. She was happy, and not even the logical thoughts about what it was going to mean to let someone into her life were enough to dissuade her from that.

Her man was still deep in slumber and after a few more minutes of cuddling, Dakota toyed with the idea of waking him up with a hand, or her mouth, on his cock. But the urgent need to use the bathroom won out, and she slipped from his arms and out of the bed.

After using the washroom, Dakota padded down the stairs and found the T-shirt she'd discarded on the couch the day before. She popped it over her head and moved to the window. Outside, the sun was only just starting to creep over the mountain, casting everything in the dim, gray light of dawn.

They'd been so consumed by each other that almost an entire day had gone by, and they hadn't even noticed. Dakota smiled and wrapped her arms around her waist, giving herself a gentle hug before stepping away to find her phone.

She'd been offline too long, and she couldn't remember whether she'd scheduled a post for her followers. As blissful as she felt, she still had a business to run, and if she was quick, she could get something posted, answer a few comments, and slip back into bed before her slumbering bear woke up.

By the time she retrieved her phone and logged on, some of the peace she'd been feeling had slipped away as the busyness of reality took over. Her inbox was overflowing with unanswered messages and questions from followers. Her social media channels had hundreds of comments wondering where the next video was and speculating on why it was late. Because, Dakota realized with a groan, it *was* late. A quick check told her that she'd completely forgotten to schedule her video on an ombre eyeshadow technique that she'd prerecorded.

It wasn't like her to forget. Then again, it wasn't like her to have her senses on overdrive because she'd walked face-first into her fated mate, scrambling her brain and throwing her for a massive loop, either. There was no point dwelling on it. She fetched the video from the virtual cloud storage where she stored her material and uploaded it quickly, along with a note apologizing for the delay. She didn't bother coming up with an excuse because she knew from experience that people saw right through bullshit. The reason that *Fuchsia* was so successful was because despite the fact that she kept her identity a secret and disguised her voice, she was completely authentic with her followers. Every other part of how she interacted with people was real, and they could sense that. Of course, Dakota wished she could be one hundred percent real with them, but her safety and privacy had to be her number one priority.

Her gaze drifted toward the stairs that led to her sleeping mate.

How on earth was she going to protect her privacy with him? It was still so early, and she was so new to the whole *mating thing*, but it didn't seem possible that she could keep secrets from Konner. *Should she?*

Her instincts told her it wasn't necessary. That he would protect her, because that's what mates do. But…something still held her back. Besides, not all decisions had to be made at once. She'd made enough big life changes for now. Revealing her true identity could wait for another day.

Before she powered off her phone, Dakota checked her personal messages. There were three missed calls and half a dozen text messages, all from Ivy.

She didn't bother listening to the voice messages and skipped straight to the texts.

> What happened? He's your mate, right?

> Are you okay?

> Dakota!

> Just let me know if it all went well.

> I'm going to assume it's all good and you're holed up somewhere having amazing sex.

> But if you're not, you need to tell me.

> CALL ME!

She laughed and shook her head. It was nice that Ivy cared. Dakota had never had a friend like her. Hell, she'd never had a friend at all. Not a real one, anyway. Not one she could be totally herself with. Ivy didn't know about Dakota's background, but she didn't care either. Almost everyone in Predator Peak had a history of some kind, and there was a general understanding that the past didn't define you. It was one of the things Dakota loved about the town and had made it even easier for her to fit in and start building a life.

To put her friend's mind at ease, Dakota tapped out a quick text.

> I'm fine. More than fine. I get it now.

She grinned when, a moment later, the phone rang, just the way she knew it would.

The space next to him was empty when Konner finally opened his eyes. He hadn't even heard Dakota slip out of bed. He hadn't slept that deeply in years, maybe ever.

He could hear the soft murmur of her voice downstairs, and the space in his chest where he'd felt the yearning and the pull when they'd been apart was warm. He could feel her nearness, and his bear was content.

In fact, every part of him, from his toes to his balls to the top of his head, felt amazing. A bone-deep contentment settled over him, and he stretched his arms up overhead and relished the satisfaction of claiming his mate.

He hadn't planned to claim her the way he had. Hell, Konner had never planned to claim a mate at all. Let alone a *cat*. But he'd do it again and again and again because it was the only thing he could have done at that moment.

Since claiming her, and finally sealing their bond, it was as if a fog had lifted from his mind. Once more, Konner could think straight and now that he had perfect clarity, he could finally figure out his next move.

He sat up against the headboard and reached over to the bedside table where his phone lay, powered off. As much as he would like to stay holed up with Dakota, kissing her, exploring her, and making her cry out in ecstasy over and over again for the rest of his days, he couldn't ignore the threat hanging over both of their heads. The night before, he'd vowed to keep her safe and he'd meant it. Bear shifters were known for their intensely protective nature, and when it came to their mates... any man would be a fool to come between them.

Konner would die before letting anything happen to Dakota.

He swallowed hard against the desire to be completely honest with her. As much as he craved being fully open with his mate, Konner knew in his heart that by keeping the truth from her, he was protecting her.

He opened his text messages and fired off an update to King.

> Found a trace by the border. Heading into Alaska tonight. Will get her.

The lie would buy him a little more time, but not much. Now that he was thinking clearly, he'd be able to come up with a more permanent solution. One that would not only keep his mate safe but also give his mother and sister the freedom they deserved. He had the beginning of an idea. He'd vowed to keep Dakota safe. But that didn't mean he wasn't going to protect his mother and sister, too.

As if Cressa knew he was thinking of her, his phone vibrated with an incoming text from his little sister.

> Where are you? Mom is losing it.

Konner rolled his eyes. His sister had a tendency to be dramatic, and given he'd recently spoken to his mother, he doubted very much there was any reason to panic. Still, after years of living with the Kings breathing down their necks, there was no way he could ignore it.

He pressed the button to call her, and his little sister answered on the first ring.

"Where are you?"

"Hi. It's nice to hear from you, too."

"Seriously, Konner. Mom's freaking out."

He could tell by her voice that this was more than just dramatics. Konner swallowed hard.

"She is? Seriously?"

"Yes. Seriously."

He sat up at full attention. "Why? What's going on?"

"It's King."

Konner's blood ran cold.

"Well, not King exactly," Cressa clarified. "But it's Sam, King's dumbass sidekick."

Konner released the breath he'd been holding. Not that having King's lackey lurking around was much better than the Mafia king himself, but it was something.

"What about Sam?"

"He's been following Mom. Nothing too obvious," Cressa continued. "But obvious enough, you know?"

Konner nodded. He walked to the window and stared out into the woods beyond the house. Of course there were risks to having his family in such an isolated town like Predator Peak, but at the moment it seemed like a much better option than leaving them alone with no one to watch out for them in the city. Konner hadn't been in the mountains for long, but it didn't take much to see that the dangers of the city far outnumbered those in Predator Peak.

"I know," he said. "Why didn't Mom tell me herself? I just spoke with her."

"She doesn't want to worry you, Konner."

He let that sink in. It was *he* who didn't want to worry his mother. She'd spent far too long worrying in her life. About them, about their father, about how or whether they'd ever be free of King's control. It was too much.

"Mom's not stupid," Cressa continued. "She knows why you're working for King, and she feels really guilty."

"Guilty?" Konner's head snapped up. "Why on earth would Mom feel guilty about what I'm doing?"

"She feels responsible for everything. For Dad, and the debt. For not leaving him when she had the chance." His sister's voice took on an uncharacteristically soft tone. "She thinks it's her fault that you're messed up with them right now. If something happened to you, I don't know—"

"Nothing is going to happen to me." Konner scrubbed a hand over his face. "We need to focus on keeping the two of you safe."

"How on earth are we going to do that? You know King has men everywhere. And if I didn't know better, I'd think he was checking up on you."

"No." Konner shook his head, unwilling to believe that King would go after his mother and sister just because he hadn't produced the Mafia princess yet. "It's fine. I'm almost finished with him for good, okay? I just need a bit more time to work it out." An idea started to take shape in his head. "Can you try to lay low until I do?"

It was a huge ask for his little sister, who spent most of her free time when she wasn't busy trying to earn her degree in education in the nightclubs, doing the exact opposite of laying low. Cressa was very much a work hard, party even harder kind of girl, so when she agreed to his ask, Konner knew the situation was a lot more serious than even she was letting on.

"I promise," he said seriously. "I'll figure this out, Cressa. And soon."

"So, it's good?"

Dakota had just spent the last few minutes telling Ivy all—well, almost all—the details of what had happened with Konner, including the fact that they were now sealed together as mates.

"It's *so* good." She almost laughed at the dreamy tone in

her voice, but it didn't matter that she was acting like a love-struck fool. She was. "Everything about it, about *him*. It's so, *so* good."

"I told you." Ivy laughed on the other end of the phone. "Now, aren't you glad you didn't fight it? When I think of the days Nolan and I lost to our stubbornness...well, it's crazy. There's really no point in fighting fate. Especially when it's all going to turn out so amazing in the end anyway."

Dakota couldn't argue with that.

"So, what's next?"

Ivy's question caught her off guard. She looked around the kitchen, her eyes landing on the coffeepot. "I guess I'm going to make coffee next."

Dakota's answer sent her friend into hysterics. "I meant," she said when she was able to control herself. "What happens next with the two of you? And you know I don't mean breakfast."

Dakota rolled her eyes, even though Ivy couldn't see her, and set to work filling the coffeepot anyway. Maybe that's not what Ivy meant, but she did need some coffee after a night without much sleep. Even if the reason for the lack of rest was a *very* good one. She grinned to herself as she filled the pot.

"So?" Ivy prompted. "Are you guys going to live happily ever after, having all kinds of...are they cubs or kittens?"

The thought stopped her, and Dakota froze. She hadn't thought about children at all, let alone what they'd *be*. There was a lot she didn't know about mating, let alone mating with a bear. Hell, she still didn't know much about her mate. "Slow down, Mama." She shook her head and poured the water into the coffeemaker before going in search of grounds. "It's still new. *Really* new. Right now, we're just enjoying each other."

"I bet you are."

Dakota could picture Ivy's eyebrows wiggling, and she laughed. "And we're getting to know each other. And there's so much to know." She located the grounds and scooped a few spoonfuls into the basket. "In fact, remember when I thought someone was following me?"

"Of course I remember." The laughter vanished from Ivy's voice. "Did you tell Konner about it? He'll be able to—"

"It was him." Dakota cut her off. "Isn't that crazy? All this time, I was afraid that…well, it doesn't matter what I was afraid of because it was Konner who was following me. Isn't that—"

"Scary."

"Well, I was going to say it was kind of a crazy coincidence, but—"

"Dakota, that's crazy." There was no trace of humor left in Ivy's voice at all. "And not in a funny way. In a totally fucking creepy way."

Dakota dropped the spoon to the counter and flicked the coffeepot on. She leaned back against the counter and adjusted the phone to her ear. "How is it creepy?" Even as she asked the question, a flicker of doubt sparked in her gut. "When he saw me for the first time, he said he thought there was a connection, but he couldn't be sure and so he—"

"Followed you for weeks just to be sure?" Ivy blew out a breath. "That's creepy. You don't think so?"

"No, I…" Dakota couldn't finish the statement because, in truth, the whole thing was a little unsettling. "Okay, maybe it is a little strange," she admitted. "But it doesn't matter now because when I'm with him I feel…*good*." She closed her eyes and sucked in a deep breath. "So good, Ivy. Unlike anything I've ever felt before. And it's more than that, too. I feel safe with him. He wouldn't hurt me."

The memory of him kissing his way down her body, promising to never hurt her and vowing to always protect her, filled her mind. Those hadn't been just words. It hadn't been mere seduction. It had been so much more. With her entire soul, she believed him. Whether or not he'd followed her secretly no longer mattered. The only thing that mattered was that they were together now. He was hers, and she was his.

"He's my mate."

"Yes. He is." Ivy's voice had softened. "I'm sorry, Dakota. I didn't mean to imply anything. You know I fully support you. And if anyone understands what it's like to experience the fated mate bond, it's me."

"I know." She knew Ivy was only being a good friend and, under any other circumstance, learning that Konner had been following her for weeks *would* have been creepy. But when it came to fate and mates…well, all of a sudden, nothing seemed too out of the ordinary. "And I appreciate that you're looking out for me."

"You know I always will," Ivy said seriously. "No matter what. You're my best friend. I've got you."

A whole new sensation of warmth and love washed through her. Dakota couldn't ever remember a time in her life when she'd ever been accepted and *loved*, just for being herself. It meant more than Ivy could ever know. "Thank you."

A sound from upstairs alerted her that Konner was awake, and her body reacted with an instant state of arousal. "Ivy, I've got to go. But I promise I'll call you soon, and I really want you and Nolan to meet Konner. I mean, if we're going to be…well, I don't know what we're going to do." She laughed. "But it's important for me that you see for yourself he's a good guy."

Ivy laughed again. "And I can drill him on the whole stalking thing."

Dakota shook her head, but she didn't argue. "You can do whatever you need to do."

She ended the call and had just set her phone on the counter when her very sexy, very naked, very aroused mate appeared at the kitchen door.

Chapter Nine

"WHY ARE WE DOING THIS AGAIN?" Konner squinted against the warm sun and made a show of trying to hide his face behind Dakota's back as they stepped out onto the front porch for the first time in days. "It's much cozier inside." He pulled her toward him. "With you." His hands slid down her back to her ass. "Naked."

She laughed and squirmed out of his grasp before turning to face him. "We've been inside for days."

"I didn't hear you complaining."

Konner wiggled his eyebrows, and she laughed again. No. She was definitely not complaining about the time they'd spent holed up in his house, making love and concreting their bond to each other. But they couldn't stay locked away from the world forever. Besides, she needed to stop by her house and get a change of clothes and her filming equipment. Her fans weren't going to wait forever for new content, and somehow, Dakota didn't think she'd be able to use her new *mate* as an excuse for not delivering.

"And sunshine is good for you." She reached for his hand and tugged him down the steps to the sidewalk.

"Sunshine is *not* good for me," Konner protested. "I'm a bear. We're nocturnal creatures."

Dakota gave him a side eye and kept walking.

"Aren't cats supposed to be nocturnal, too?" He tugged her closer and wrapped his arm around her waist while they walked. "I wouldn't have guessed you were a sun worshipper."

"I'm hardly a sun worshipper." She shook her head, but secretly thought his teasing was cute. "But I do like to get outside now and then. Especially now that spring has finally come to the mountains. I wasn't sure it would ever get here. I'm not used to such long winters growing up on the coast."

Reflexively, Dakota froze. She never told people where she was from. But as quickly as the reaction hit her, it disappeared. Konner was her mate. There was no reason he shouldn't know that's where she'd spent her childhood. She still hadn't told Konner the whole truth about her past or her family, but they had shared some details about their lives. She'd told him she was an only child, raised by her father in what was largely a loveless home and as soon as she could, she'd taken off. In turn, Konner told her that he had a younger sister, his own father passed away and he remained close to his mother. She loved the idea of a close family, even if the concept was a foreign one.

"Where did you grow up?" She tipped her head toward him as they walked slowly down the street toward her house.

"Would you believe, I grew up on the coast, too? Maybe we were neighbors?"

"I doubt that very much." Dakota laughed. "But that would explain why you're so averse to the sunlight. The winters in Vancouver are *so* dreary."

Konner stopped and spun her into his arms. "You are the only reason I want to stay holed up inside." He kissed her deeply. "But I'm all for being outside if it means I can strip you naked and see how gorgeous your beautiful body is with the sun shining down."

His words sent heat through her, directly between her legs. "Maybe later we can go out to the woods and find a private little spot in the trees?"

A growl of approval rumbled from his chest, and he kissed her again. If they weren't careful, they wouldn't make it to the forest before stripping each other naked right there in the middle of the street. Not for the first time, Dakota could see the value in the way wolf shifters treated a new mate pairing. The couple would retreat to a *nest* somewhere, where they could be alone together to cement their bond to each other. The process could take anywhere from a few days to a few years apparently, and from the way Ivy told it, they basically spent the entire time naked and fucking.

It sounded like a pretty good deal to Dakota, but cats and bears didn't instinctively need the *nesting* period. And even if they did, Dakota would likely feel too much pressure to provide content for her followers. Like it or not, that's still how she paid the bills.

Dakota managed to tear herself away from Konner and once more started to pull him down the street toward her house.

He pretended to pout, before catching up and squeezing her hand in his. "How about on the way to your place, we stop and get a coffee? After all, we never really did get a chance to finish our drinks the last time we were there."

He laughed but his words reminded her that Konner already knew where she lived. *Was that because he'd been following her or because of his instinctive pull toward her, the same way she'd known where to find him?*

She'd tried not to let it bother her, but Ivy's reaction when she'd told her friend that it had been Konner who'd been following her had stuck with her. It's not that it bothered her, or that she didn't trust him—she did. Instinctively through the bond, Dakota knew he wouldn't hurt her. But there was something else. Unable to take another step, Dakota pulled him off the street onto a bench. "Remember when you told me it was you that was following me all that time?"

Confused, it took Konner a moment to realize Dakota wasn't stopping him to make out.

She watched as the smile slipped off his face, matching her serious tone.

"I am so sorry about that, Dakota." He took her hands in his and squeezed. "I need you to believe me when I tell you I didn't mean to scare you. If I could do that over again, I—"

"I do believe you. But the thing is, I'm starting to wonder if it *was* you I was scared of."

Konner shook his head. "What do you mean?"

She looked down at their hands before blowing out a breath. "I didn't want to tell you this because I didn't think it was anything and I didn't want to worry you. But—"

"What is it?"

In an instant, Konner was in protector mode. He sat up straight, his chest out and although he still held her hands gently in his own, she could feel the tension as it radiated off him in waves. Dakota knew it wasn't the intention, but in that moment, she felt even safer than she had before. There was no doubt that this man would protect her against any threat. Real or imaginary. And hopefully, that's all this latest concern was: an imaginary threat.

Still, she needed to tell him. "I've been getting some strange messages," she told him. "On my posts and privately in my inbox."

"What kind of messages?" His voice was low, full of concern.

He'd already seen all her posts as Fuchsia, and she'd tried her best to explain what it was she did for a living and how she earned money through affiliate links and sponsored posts. Konner had obviously made an effort, but it was clear he still didn't fully understand what she did. He had, however, commented on how public she was and how that concerned him.

"Did someone threaten you?"

Dakota shook her head. "Not directly, no. It's more… well…there's something about me that you should know."

Konner sat and listened carefully while Dakota opened up to him about who she really was. Even though none of what she told him was news to him, listening to her explain how she'd been emotionally and often physically abused since she was a young child made him crazy. His bear was out for blood. If King had the misfortune to present himself at that very moment, there was no doubt that Konner would rip him apart. And he wouldn't feel the slightest bit of remorse, either. All the hell the man had put Konner's family through was nothing compared to the abuse of his mate.

"Just over a year ago," Dakota continued, "I learned that my father had promised me in marriage to Dominic Dufort, a panther shifter from an even more violent Mafia family in Florida." She looked up into Konner's eyes, and he saw the fear in her gaze. "He's an awful man, Konner." She shook her head. "The way he'd look at me…the things he said he'd do to me… I just…"

"Ssh." Konner rubbed his hand over her leg to reassure her. "You don't have to say it out loud."

She attempted a small smile. "I knew I couldn't let it

happen." She shivered as she spoke, despite the warmth of the sun. "I had to run away and start over. And I did." The smile began to reach her eyes. "I changed my name and started Fuchsia, and everything I have, I earned on my own. Away from them."

"You've done an amazing job." She really had. Despite the fact that she held a very public persona, she'd been difficult to track down. Difficult, but not impossible. If he failed to return her, Konner knew King wasn't going to give up. He'd only send someone else for her, and that person *would* find her. Unless he did something about it. "You're incredibly strong."

"No." She shook her head. "That's the thing. I'm not. I mean, I should be—I'm a mountain lion shifter, for goodness' sake. But all those years living like I did, I grew weak and timid. And then, lately, when I thought I was being followed…"

He swallowed hard, so angry at himself for scaring her.

"I should have been able to defend myself, but instead, I just hid."

He gritted his teeth and swallowed hard against the growing rage he had for King and his men for making his fierce mate feel anything but.

"My real name is Angelica King, but that's not who I am." She set her jaw and straightened her shoulders.

It was easy to see how she'd been able to survive such awful things as a child, and still have the strength to run away and start over all on her own. His mate was fierce even if she didn't see it. There was no doubt about that.

"But I'm Dakota Hill now."

"Thank you for sharing that with me." Konner cupped her cheek in his hand. "You're safe now. And I promise I'll do everything in my power to keep you safe. You don't need to worry about them anymore, Dakota."

"You don't know them. They won't quit." She shook her head and tried to look away, but Konner held her face in place and looked deep into her eyes.

"I do know—" He stopped himself. As much as he hated the secrets between them, he needed to keep this one. Just for a little bit longer. At least until he knew she was safe for good. "I know men like him," he corrected himself. "Cruel, heartless men who only look out for themselves. I've had to deal with them, too."

Dakota closed her eyes. "So you know."

"I do." He waited until she looked at him again. "And I know how to protect you from them, Dakota. I promise you, you're safe with me, and you always will be. I need you to believe me."

She nodded. "I do believe you. But I think they might have found me."

Her words caused his blood to run cold. Konner froze; his spine stiffened, and he was immediately on alert. *Did King double-cross him and send someone after him? Maybe he didn't buy all of Konner's excuses after all?* He'd let his defenses down and now... *Fuck.*

"What do you mean?" His head was on a swivel as he scanned their surroundings. *How could he have been so stupid?* They just sat there in the middle of the street, right out in the open where anyone could see them and pick them off. King's men could be watching them right now, planning on how to best kill him and snatch Dakota before he even knew what happened. "Are they following us?"

"I've been getting messages." Dakota pulled her phone out of her pocket and clicked on the screen.

"Messages? What kind of messages?"

"Look." She thrust the phone at him.

It took Konner a moment to realize he was looking at the private messages on Fuchsia's account.

. . .

I can't believe I found you.

I know who you are.

I'd like to meet.

I need to see you.

Konner read the messages twice through before looking up in confusion. "These were sent to Fuchsia?"

She nodded. "I get messages all the time, but there's something different about these."

"And you don't know who...PrairieGold15 is?"

She shook her head. "They've never commented before and then, all of a sudden, all of these. Do you think he's been the one watching me? Do you think he's out there right now?"

Konner's mind worked overtime to make sense of everything. It wasn't like King or his men to send messages that would alert her to them. They would just show up unannounced. It didn't feel like King, which meant it was a different, unknown threat—and that was even worse, because he didn't know what to expect. They could be dealing with a dangerous stalker. More likely it was some stupid kid who had more bravery than brains, hiding behind his keyboard. But there was no way to know, and when it came to Dakota, he wasn't taking any chances.

"Come on." He stood and held out a hand for Dakota. "I need to get you home. There's something I need to do."

Whoever was sending those messages probably wasn't a real threat. Or at least, not a threat that Konner couldn't easily manage. King was still the real threat, and all this latest issue did was shine a light on it. Dakota wasn't going to be truly safe until he took care of matters, and there was only one way to do it.

He hated to leave his new mate alone, and under any other circumstances, he wouldn't. But this wasn't an ordinary situation, and it was the only way to take care of the issue once and for all.

Chapter Ten

IT HAD BEEN two days since Konner made her promise to stay with Ivy and Nolan and left town. She felt his absence keenly, like a cramp in her gut and ache in her chest that wouldn't subside no matter what she did to try to relieve it.

She'd tried to keep herself busy by recording new videos and making content that she could schedule for the next few weeks, but her heart wasn't in it. Mostly she moped around Ivy and Nolan's new house until finally Ivy had enough.

"Okay, let's go." She stood at the end of the couch. With her hands on her hips and her large belly sticking out, she was an even more imposing presence than usual.

"Go where?" Dakota tugged the blanket up to her chin.

"Get up," Ivy ordered. "We're getting out of this house."

Dakota shook her head. "Konner said I should stay—"

"With us." Ivy cut her off. "And we agreed to let you stay here because you're my best friend and I love you. But we told Konner you would stay *with* us, not necessarily that you'd stay in the house. So let's go."

Before Dakota could protest again, Ivy reached down and pulled the blanket off. "I need some fresh air," Ivy said. "We're going for a walk. And before you protest, yes, Nolan's coming, so you don't need to count on a pregnant wolf shifter to protect you."

"I don't need protecting." Dakota sat up and exposed her razor-sharp claws from the tips of her fingers. She wiggled her eyebrows when Ivy laughed and put her claws away.

"You don't need to tell me that." Ivy shook her head. "In fact, I'd bet on you over any random internet creep any day. Konner's just being an overprotective bear." She groaned. "So typical of bears. Come on."

Dakota wished she'd really meant what she'd said. Although she would like to think that she didn't need protecting because she was a fierce mountain lion shifter, she'd spent way more time frightened and in hiding than she was proud of. Still, if it came right down to it, could she hold her own?

Not that there was any point arguing with her friend. Before Konner had left her, she'd been able to sense his concern, and she hadn't missed how he'd taken Nolan aside to have a talk with him. Whatever Konner was worried about, Dakota could tell it was real and not just an overprotective new mate.

Overprotective or not, it was the situation she was in, so there was no point stirring up more trouble. Besides, she could think of worse ways to spend an afternoon than walking with two of her closest friends.

A few minutes later, the threesome set off in the warm spring sunshine for a gentle walk. To her surprise, Dakota found herself enjoying herself with her friends instead of obsessing about her mate's absence. They made their way to Predator Peak's Main Street and while Nolan waited outside, Ivy and

Dakota popped in and out of the shops, until finally, Nolan had hit his shopping limit.

"No more shops, Ivy." Nolan shook his head, and Dakota tried not to laugh. "I can't face it."

"There was actually—"

"No."

Ivy laughed when, exasperated, Nolan crossed his arms over his chest.

"I'm kidding." She stood on her tiptoes and kissed him on the cheek. "You've been very patient. How about a beer?"

Nolan's eyes lit up like a kid on Christmas morning. "You mean it?"

"Is that okay with you, Dakota?"

"Absolutely."

Nolan had already started walking in the direction of the Well.

"This baby could use a snack anyway, and Ruby will be excited to see you."

Just as she'd predicted, Ivy's seven-year-old niece ran full speed toward them, the moment they set foot into the pub.

Nolan caught her easily in his arms and swung her around in the air before she could crash into Ivy. "Hey, kiddo. You gotta be careful around your auntie until the baby's born. You'll knock her over."

"Silly Uncle Nolan. I'm not strong enough to knock her over." She shook her head and rolled her eyes until Nolan set her down.

"You might be surprised, Ruby." Ivy gave her niece a hug. "I don't really have the best balance these days."

"Dad says you're going to get even bigger before the baby's born." Ruby's eyes grew wide, and she looked at Dakota for confirmation. "Is that true?"

Dakota nodded seriously. "She's going to be massive." She held her arms out wide until Ivy smacked her.

"Just wait."

"No way." Dakota shook her head. "I mean, never say never. But I'm safe to say not right now. Everything is still way too new."

Before her, Nolan choked on a laugh. "Right. We don't know anything about that."

He let Ruby lead them through the pub to a table near the front where she had her pencil crayons and an art pad spread out. In almost any other town, it would be unusual to see a child so at home in a pub, but not in Predator Peak. Ruby and her dad lived upstairs, and when Jager wasn't trying to be sure his little girl was getting an education, she could either be found playing in the woods or in the bar itself.

More and more, the education part of Ruby's life was getting harder for Jager to handle. Ivy helped out as much as she could, and there was a local woman, Josephine, who was a retired teacher and volunteered her skills to help out with Ruby and some of the other children in Predator Peak. But the job was proving to be more than the older woman could comfortably handle these days, and with Ivy about to get even busier when the baby came, even Dakota could see that there was going to be a need for a real teacher, and maybe even a school in Predator Peak soon.

"What are you working on?" she asked the little girl as she slid into the booth and peeked at Ruby's drawings. "These are really good."

"I know."

"Ruby," Ivy chastised. "You're supposed to say thank you."

"But I do know they're good." Ruby shrugged and focused on Dakota again. "I want to draw all the trees in the forest," she told Dakota. "And then when I'm done, I'll draw the flowers and maybe the mushrooms. But Dad doesn't want me—"

"What don't I want you doing?"

"Eating the mushrooms in the forest?"

"Definitely not." Jager grinned and placed a mug of beer in front of Nolan, who accepted it gratefully. "I didn't know what you'd want," he said to Dakota. "And you…" He tilted his head in the direction of his sister. "I assume you want food."

"You assume correctly." Ivy laughed. "A grilled cheese sandwich with a side of dill pickles."

"That's not on the menu."

Ivy shrugged. "Boris will make it."

Jager shook his head, because he knew she was right, and looked at Dakota for her order.

"Just an iced tea for me."

"I'll be right back with that." Jager ruffled Ruby's hair. "And it's on the house if you can get this one to do her math worksheets."

"You know it's on the house anyway." Ivy snort-laughed. "But yes, I'm sure Ruby will be happy to show us how good she is at her math work."

Jager shot his sister a look, but Dakota saw the smile on his face as he walked away. Not for the first time, she felt a shot of jealousy at their relationship. She'd always wanted a sibling growing up. Maybe childhood would have been different had there been someone to share it with. Maybe it would have been tolerable.

Lost in thought, Dakota wasn't paying attention as Ivy started to help Ruby with her math work. It wasn't until Nolan nudged her under the table that she focused on her surroundings.

"Do you know that guy?"

At once, Dakota was on guard. Her spine stiffened and the hair on the back of her neck stood up as she scanned the room, her gaze finally landing on the man Nolan was referring to.

"He was looking this way," Nolan said under his breath. "I

don't think I've ever seen him before, but there's something about him that's—"

"Who are we talking about?" Ivy spun around in her chair and openly stared at the man, who smiled in their direction.

There was nothing threatening about him, but given everything that had happened in the last few months, never mind the last week, to say that Dakota was wary would be putting it very mildly.

"Oh!" Ivy spun around and stared at Dakota. "Do you know him? He looks…" She turned in her seat *again*.

This time, Dakota elbowed her in the ribs. "Turn around," she hissed. "I don't know him, and I don't want to attract attention."

Next to her, Nolan stiffened. "Konner told me you were nervous about some comments you were getting. Don't worry, Dakota. If he tries anything, I'll rip his head off."

"Thank—"

"You're not ripping anyone's head off, Nolan." Ivy looked between them. "And what the hell is this about comments? What kind of comments? I thought you said it was Konner who was following you. I still don't think that's okay, but we all know he isn't going to—"

"Auntie Ivy, you said hell."

All three adults turned to look at Ruby, who sat quietly, her math sheet in front of her, a devious grin on her face.

"You know quite well that I'm an adult, Ruby. And adults can say adult words."

Ruby giggled, and Ivy shook her head before turning around to stare at the stranger again. "Who is he? He looks…" She faced Dakota, who finished the statement.

"He looks familiar," she said almost to herself. "I feel like I should know him but I've never—"

"It looks like we're going to know him," Ivy said. "He's coming over."

Konner had been traveling for over twenty-four hours without rest by the time he crossed the border into Alaska. It was after ten at night, but the closer they got to the summer solstice, the longer the days got. Instead of having the cover of darkness as he arrived at the edge of town, there was a low, dusky light that illuminated his surroundings and cast everything in an eerie, yet almost mystical glow.

While he traveled, the semblance of a plan had formulated. Given more time, he might have come up with something a little more solid, but he didn't have more time, so he had to do the best he could.

The most important thing was that he finish this. For good.

King was never going to stop looking for his daughter. Not if he'd promised her in what equated to a business arrangement. He had no idea what he'd traded her for, and he didn't want to know what King thought his daughter's life was worth. It didn't matter.

The only thing that mattered was making sure she was safe. And there was only one way to do that. Angelica King needed to die.

Given everything that had happened in the last few weeks, Dakota should have been terrified as the stranger approached, but she was oddly at ease. Maybe it was the fact that she was flanked by Nolan and Ivy in a busy pub full of people who would all jump to her defense without a moment of hesitation. But it was more than that. There was something oddly familiar about the man.

She watched as he approached, and when Nolan tried to jump up from the table to stop him from getting any closer,

Dakota put a hand on his arm. "It's okay." She nodded in her friend's direction and held out a hand to the man. "Do I know you?"

He shook his head and brushed his mop of golden hair away from his face. "I know this is going to sound strange, but I think I'm your brother."

Next to her, Ivy gasped and on the other side, Nolan growled deep in his throat, ready to come to her aid. But Dakota still didn't feel threatened. "Sorry." She shook her head sadly. "I don't have a brother." She stopped herself from offering up any more information about her life. Not even her best friends knew much about her past besides the basics.

"I know this sounds crazy."

That didn't even begin to describe it.

"My name is Knox," he continued. "Knox Ward. My mother is Celeste Ward."

Celeste.

The world tilted, and she pressed both her hands on the table in front of her in an effort to steady herself. "Your mother is…" She couldn't bring herself to say the name she hadn't heard in years. Dakota had only been four years old when her mom went to the store and never came home. When she asked her father, he yelled at her as if it were her fault her mother was gone. It was also the first time he'd ever raised a hand to her. He forbid her from speaking her name, and it didn't take long for a confused and scared young girl to learn it was easier to forget about the mother who'd abandoned her than to anger her father.

"I'm sorry if this is coming out of the blue," Knox spoke quickly. "I tried to message you. At least I think it was you. The messages were sort of cryptic because I wasn't sure it was you, and…well, you're not a very easy person to find."

Dakota shook her head. "That was you?" For the first time since he'd approached, Dakota was on high alert. This man had found her through Fuchsia. And not *her*, but Angelica. Which meant…he knew who she was. Her spine stiffened, and she scanned the room, looking for her father. Or worse, Dominic.

"I think you should go." Nolan had stood up and was now between Knox and Dakota, whose mind was spinning too fast to make sense of anything.

He knew who she was.

He knew her mother.

He was her…

"Wait." She slid from her seat at the table and put her hand on Nolan's arm. "There's something about…" Words failed her when she looked into his eyes. That was it. That was what was so familiar.

Knox had the same golden eyes that she did. That her mother did.

"You are my brother." It wasn't a question. As crazy as it was, Dakota felt it in her soul when she looked into the familiar eyes. She'd never known anyone but her mother to have eyes like she did. It was one of the only things she remembered about her mom. And it was the one thing her father hated most about her, because she reminded him of his wife who'd left him. Knox had the same eyes.

"Dakota?" Ivy stood next to her, her face lined in concern. "Do you want—"

"It's okay," she said without looking away from Knox. "This is—"

"We're gonna need proof."

All the adults looked down to see Ruby standing next to Nolan, her little hands on her hips, doing her best to look mighty. She glared up at Knox. "How do I know you're not *my* brother?"

Dakota grinned and turned to Ivy, but her best friend wasn't smiling.

"I agree," Ivy said. "We need proof."

Instead of looking offended or brushing Ruby off as an annoyance, Knox chuckled and addressed the little girl. "You're right," he said. "I suppose some proof is probably warranted." He pulled his wallet from the back pocket of his jeans and pulled a photograph out. "I can't prove that I'm not *your* brother," he said to Ruby. "But I think this might prove that I am yours." He turned to Dakota while he spoke and handed her the photograph.

Her breath caught in her throat and her heart squeezed as she looked at the image. She remembered the day it was taken. It was her fourth birthday, and her mother had dressed them in matching sweaters she'd knitted herself. She sat on her mother's lap, her head leaned back on her mother's chest, identical smiles on both of their faces.

Three weeks later, her mother was gone.

"Holy shit," Ivy said. "You look just like her."

She did. Her mother was about her age now when the photo was taken. The resemblance was uncanny.

Dakota touched the picture gently, as if she could feel her mom through the magic of time.

"This photo was framed on Mom's bedside table. She used to talk about you all the time."

A tear slipped down Dakota's cheek as his words sunk in. "Used to?"

Knox's lips turned down into a frown. "She died two years ago."

It shouldn't have hurt. After all, she'd lost her mother years ago. Yet, the news struck her fresh, and a sob escaped her.

"Why don't we leave you two alone for a few minutes?" Ivy squeezed her arm reassuringly. "We'll be right over there if you need us, okay?"

Dakota nodded, but she couldn't take her eyes off the

picture of her mother until Knox led her gently back to her seat.

He took the one across from her and rested his hands on the tabletop. "I know this is all a lot."

"You have no idea." Dakota took a deep breath. "I guess I just thought she was dead."

He nodded slowly. "I think that was the point," he said softly. "She would want you to know how much she loved you, Dakota." He hesitated and glanced around before adding, "Should I call you—"

"Dakota." She cut him off sharply. "That's my name." She narrowed her eyes, and a small hiss escaped her lips as she remembered that this man—her brother—had found her despite the great care she'd taken to hide herself. He knew who she was and that was dangerous. Especially considering she didn't know anything about Knox.

"Got it." He nodded. "I won't say anything."

"I want to know exactly how you found me, and why. And those cryptic messages you sent me." She shook her head. "They were terrifying. I didn't know…I thought…"

"I'm sorry about those," he said. "I wasn't sure if it was really you, and I didn't want to give too much away in case it wasn't. I've never really done anything like this before."

Dakota nodded. "I want to know all that." She took a deep breath and filled her lungs before exhaling slowly. "But first, I need to know everything about her. I need to…" Tears choked her words.

When Knox reached across the table and took her hand, it felt like the most natural thing in the world.

He squeezed and gave her a soft smile. "It would be my pleasure to tell you everything I can. I think she'd like that a lot."

Chapter Eleven

KONNER DIDN'T STOP to rest until he was sure everything was in place. He'd done his research before crossing the border and found a small remote town in Alaska where there was a history of women disappearing. It made him sick to think of what had happened to all those poor young women, but he couldn't let himself feel too much, because Angelica was about to be one of them.

The first thing he did was plant some of her clothing, including a hat that he'd been sure had strands of Dakota's hair stuck in it, that he'd snuck from her house before leaving, on the edge of town, just off the highway where it would be found if anyone bothered to look. Then he made his way to the nearest bar, where he started asking around, pretending to be a concerned cousin of a missing woman. He told anyone who would listen what she'd been wearing the last time she was seen. He was careful not to give too many details, but just enough to plant the seed that there was *another* missing young woman.

Once he'd planted the seed in the pub, he moved on to the local shops and finally to the police department, where he was told that he was welcome to file a missing person's report, but that it wasn't likely to amount to anything.

If Angelica had been hitchhiking on that particular stretch of road, either the wild animals had gotten her, or, more likely, according to law enforcement, the same guy who'd been terrorizing young women for decades up there had found a new victim.

Konner tried to swallow his disgust at the officers who appeared more interested in scrolling through their phones and comparing hunting stories while they drank stale coffee than they were solving actual crimes. They spoke candidly about the dozens of women who'd gone missing over the years around their town, and how the perpetrator, whomever he was, never left a trace. Every lead they'd ever had led to a dead end. The story was corroborated by everyone he came across who bothered to speak to him about it at all.

"Even been featured on *Dateline*," the cashier at the grocery told him with a trace of what sounded a little too much like pride. "The highway's been dubbed the Highway of Heartbreak. Ya know, 'cause of all the missing—"

"Yeah. I got it."

Konner shook his head and made note of everything he heard that would back up his story of Angelica's disappearance.

On his way out of town in the late twilight hours, he placed an anonymous call to the police station, reporting the sighting of a woman's discarded belongings on the edge of town.

After experiencing the apathy of the townspeople, never mind local law enforcement, Konner didn't have much faith that the *evidence* would be tested for DNA. But if they were, the strands of hair should be enough to prove it was Angelica who'd been the latest victim of the Highway of Heartbreak, and King would have no choice but to believe the story he was about to tell him.

There were definite holes in his story, but he hoped like hell King would believe it. He was counting on the man not filing an actual police report. And considering the last thing King ever wanted was police attention on him in any way, Konner was confident he wouldn't.

He shifted into his bear and ran hard back into Canadian territory before he found a spot with cell service to make the call.

"Dead?"

Konner swallowed hard. "I can't know for sure, sir. I didn't see her body, but all the evidence points to that conclusion, yes." He held his breath, knowing that King wouldn't take the news at face value.

"What is this Highway of Heartbreak you're talking about?"

"You can look it up online," Konner said. "I had to. But apparently, it's a thing up there where young women disappear. The sheriff was pretty sure that was the case with Angelica, too. And not to worry," he added quickly. "I was careful to keep my questions vague. There shouldn't be any unwanted attention coming your way."

Except that, it's your daughter who's missing.

Konner felt sick knowing that the fact that Angelica was *dead* was going to be the least of King's concerns. Primarily, the man was worried about his image and his bottom line. If Konner knew him the way he suspected he did, King would move quickly to put this mess behind him and move on. With Angelica *dead*, he would have to refocus his energies. He already knew the man didn't have any love for his daughter; there would be no grieving—unless it was for the loss of a business deal with the promised marriage to Dominic.

"Fuck," King said after a moment. "She's dead?"

"Looks that way, sir." He exhaled slowly. "You know I

wouldn't jump to conclusions unless I was sure. I pride myself on being thorough."

"I do know that." King muttered a series of hard-to-decipher expletives under his breath. "You're a solid man, Konner. Not like that piece of shit of a father you had."

Konner gritted his teeth and swallowed hard. He'd learned a long time ago it was easier not to rise to the bait.

"I've always been able to trust you to get the job done."

That was because you held my family's debt over my head.

"Of course, sir."

"We'll discuss the next steps when you get back."

"That's the thing, sir." He scrubbed his hand over his face and plowed ahead with the request. "I think I'm going to take a few days off before I head back. These last few weeks have exhausted me. I just need to lay low and get some rest for a few days." He knew it was a risk. A big one. King would want him back in Vancouver as soon as possible. He liked to keep his lackeys close by and holidays were unheard of.

He knew he should probably just go back right away to see for himself that King bought his story and Dakota was finally safe, but the ache in his chest made it almost impossible to think. He'd already been gone too long. He needed to get back to his mate.

They'd talked for hours, and with every minute that passed, Dakota was more and more confident that Knox was her brother. He told her stories of their mother, including why she'd never come looking for Dakota. That was the hardest part to hear, but deep down, Dakota understood why she'd done what she had.

Her father was a dangerous man. She knew that well. It made sense that her mother had been subject to that same cruelty, probably worse. Celeste had done the only thing she could to save her own life by running away when she had. According to Knox, it was a decision that haunted her for the rest of her life.

"She told me all the time how she wished she'd taken you with her," Knox said. "She would never have left you if she thought your father would take it out on you."

"She had no way to know." It was true. Her father was never awful to her until after her mother was gone. Cold and unaffectionate, yes. But not cruel. That came later.

"She met my father a few months after she left, and I was born exactly nine months later." He laughed, but Dakota didn't join in.

She was trying to picture the version of her mother that she only vaguely remembered, starting over with a whole new family so soon after leaving her behind. She couldn't pretend it didn't hurt.

"Was she happy?"

The laughter fell away, but a soft smile lingered on Knox's lips. "She was. But when my father died, her light dimmed, and she was gone a few months later." Her brother reached across the table and took her hand. "I want you to know that she made me promise to find you and make sure you were safe. And happy."

"That's why you're here?"

Knox nodded. "I know this sounds strange, Dakota. But I kind of feel like I grew up with you in a way."

She sat back and raised an eyebrow.

"Mom talked about you all the time," he added. "And she kept track of you, too. There was a woman who would send her pictures and updates about you over the years. I can't remember her name, but—"

"Aunt Michelle."

Knox shrugged. "Maybe. I never knew her name."

It had to be. There was no one else. Auntie Michelle was her father's sister, and the only one in the King family who'd ever shown Dakota any affection through the years, sparse as it was. "She knew where my mother was? I can't believe she wouldn't tell me." But Dakota could believe it. Aunt Michelle had always kept her distance, and like everyone else, she was scared of her older brother.

Her mind reeled with all the information Knox was giving her. But there was still something she needed to know. "How did you find me? I was so careful."

"You were very careful."

"But if you found me…"

"No," he assured her. "They won't. The only reason I knew where to look was because…and this is going to sound stupid…I saw one of your videos."

"Fuchsia's videos?"

He nodded, his face flushing a bright pink.

"You watch makeup videos?"

Knox's head shot up, his eyes wide. "No. Well, yes. I guess that one I did. But it was a girl I was dating for a while. She was addicted to her phone. I swear, I've never met anyone who stares at their phone so much." He shook his head. "It's why we broke up, actually."

Dakota raised an eyebrow in question, but Knox got back on track.

"Anyway, one day we were lying in bed, and she was scrolling through her phone when she screamed. Turns out she'd found one of your videos. You were doing some sort of thing with eyeshadow, and she recognized your eye."

"My eye?"

"I don't know if you've noticed, but we have the same rather distinct eyes."

His smile was so disarming that Dakota forgot to be concerned that if one person was able to recognize her by her eyes alone, then maybe others would too.

"But don't worry," Knox continued. "It wasn't easy to find you after that. You've done a really good job covering your tracks. And I'm honestly not here for any other reason than to—"

A deafening roar split the air, and a second later, Knox was on his back, with a massive black bear, teeth bared, pinning him to the ground.

Chapter Twelve

KONNER MOVED PURELY ON INSTINCT. He didn't take the time to assess the situation or ask questions.

He just reacted.

It wasn't until he was on top of the stranger, his teeth bared, ready to rip his throat out for threatening his mate, that it even occurred to Konner that there might not be any threat at all.

"Konner!" Dakota's scream pierced the air, followed by the sharp slash of her claws across his face. "Stop!"

He growled and swung his massive head away. He still didn't move, but he took a moment to look down at the face of the man he'd attacked. Familiar golden eyes stared back at him. Confused, Konner looked at his mate.

She was pissed. Dakota's hands were on her hips, which at least kept her from slashing him again. *That stung.* Her eyes blazed with anger and her jaw was set.

There was more yelling as others approached, and Konner finally realized his error. He shook his head in what he hoped was an apology and as quickly as he could, without causing any more damage, made his way outside.

By the time he shifted, dressed, and returned inside the Well, things had been put back to order somewhat. At least as much as they could be. Konner noted a pile of broken tables and chairs by the door and shook his head.

Fuck.

He only barely knew Jager, but he hoped the man would accept a genuine apology and some cash to replace the broken furniture. But that would have to wait. There was only one person he was worried about at the moment, and she looked even angrier than she had a few minutes ago, if it were even possible.

Dakota stood with Nolan, Ivy, and the stranger he'd attacked. As soon as he'd walked in, she turned to face him.

Her eyes flashed gold, and she shook her head a little before stepping away from the others toward him.

"Dakota." He reached for her because he couldn't not. The last few days away from her had been torture. When she didn't pull away, he cupped her cheeks and pressed his lips to hers.

She groaned and, a second later, kissed him back.

"You're okay."

"Of course I'm okay." She smacked his chest a little, but there was no heat behind it. "But I'm still…"

"Mad?" He wiggled his eyebrows, teasing her. Just as he hoped, Dakota grinned.

"Yes," she said, but it held no conviction. "I missed you."

He kissed her again. "Fuck, I missed you, too."

Her body melted into his. As much as he wanted to scoop her up and carry her out of there where they could have a proper reunion, there were still a few matters to attend to. He growled and forced himself to step back before his animal instincts took over completely.

"So," Dakota said. "Are you going to explain exactly what the hell that was?"

Konner shook his head. "I saw you with…I just thought

maybe he was…fuck." He scrubbed a hand over his face. "Dakota, I would do anything to protect you."

Her lips twitched as she clearly tried not to smile. It was a war within herself she couldn't win. Finally, she dropped her face into her hands and sighed. "I appreciate that," Dakota said a moment later. "But clearly I don't need you to protect me."

His gut reaction was to argue. It was his job as her mate to keep her safe. He was a natural-born protector; it was in his nature.

Dakota touched his cheek, and the cuts her nails had left on his skin. "See?" She grinned. "I can protect myself."

He caught her hand in his and pressed it to his lips. "You certainly can, kitten. I never doubted you." Movement over Dakota's shoulder reminded him that as much as he wanted to be, they were not alone. "Who's the guy?"

"You're not going to believe this." She took his hand in his and led him across the short distance to where the others were waiting.

The man with the eyes so much like Dakota's stepped forward. "Konner." He extended a hand. "I'm Knox."

Konner looked at his outstretched hand and then at Dakota.

"My brother."

It had been a long day.

Hell, it had been a long few weeks.

Had it really only been that long since Konner had walked into her life and turned it upside down?

And now, a brother?

It was a lot.

A real lot.

Dakota was exhausted.

Fortunately, after their initial meeting, there were no more teeth or claws bared between Konner and Knox. But there was still tension between them. It was clear that even though Konner conceded that the family resemblance was uncanny, he didn't trust Knox. And on the flip side, Knox acted like an overprotective brother, which was ridiculous on so many levels.

Dakota had spent her entire life on her own, with no one to look out for her and now, in the course of only a few days, she had not one, but two men all but smothering her with their *protection.*

She was going to need to set them both straight.

In the morning.

First, if her reflection in the restroom mirror was anything to go off of, she needed sleep.

"You look exhausted." Ivy's reflection appeared next to her in the mirror.

She must be tired; she hadn't even heard her friend come into the ladies' room.

"I am so tired." Dakota rubbed at her eyes. "Maybe I should do a tutorial video on hiding dark circles instead of a fancy eyeliner technique."

Her best friend laughed. "I'm sure there's a demand for that, too." Ivy put her arm around Dakota's shoulder and pulled her in for a hug. "But you need to go easy on yourself right now. This is all a lot to take in."

"That's an understatement." Dakota took a breath. "I don't even begin to know how to process everything, Ivy. I mean, I've always been a loner, you know? I'm used to being alone. I *like* being alone. And now…"

"Now you have more people who love you." Ivy pulled away and looked her in the eye. "And that's never a bad thing."

No. It wasn't a bad thing. Not at all.

"It's just a lot all at once."

Ivy laughed. "I'll tell you what. Why don't we offer Knox my old cabin to sleep in for a few days? That way you and Konner can have some privacy and a little space to digest all of…" She waved her hand and ended in a shrug. "This."

Dakota threw her arms around Ivy's neck. "Thank you. I was going to offer him my place and just stay at Konner's, but I thought it might be weird to have him in my house without me there."

"It's not a big deal. The cabin is empty, and it's neutral. I'm sure it won't take you long to get to know each other, and then you can figure out what to do from there." Her smile and her offer were genuine, and Dakota was beyond grateful for both of them.

Ivy was right; it wasn't going to take her long to get to know Knox. There was already an unexpected familiarity between them, but it wasn't her and Knox she was worried about. Something told her that Konner might not warm up to her brother quite as quickly.

A little space would be good for all of them.

Chapter Thirteen

THERE WAS NO BETTER way to wake up than in Dakota's bed with his mate nuzzled up against him, her hair splayed over his chest and her hand resting dangerously close to what was already a raging hard-on. If she so much as brushed his hard cock, Konner would not be able to be held responsible for what happened next.

He desperately wanted it to happen.

He also knew she needed sleep. She'd been so tired the night before that he had to carry her up the stairs and into her bed. The moment her head hit the pillow, she'd fallen asleep. As much as he wanted to wake her now, for a proper home-coming, Konner knew he wouldn't disrupt her slumber.

Inch by inch, he slowly tried to slip out from under her without disturbing her. He'd almost made it, too, when her long fingers wrapped around his wrist.

"Where are you going?"

"I'm letting you sleep, kitten." Konner turned and pressed a soft kiss to her lips.

"I'm awake now."

He smiled. "Go back to sleep."

Her free hand wrapped around his hard cock and squeezed until he groaned. "And you're very much awake."

That was an understatement.

"Kitten…"

"I'm not going to take no for an answer." She stroked his shaft, and Konner realized very quickly that his objections were no match to her techniques of persuasion.

He crawled up the bed until he was overtop her, tenting her in with his arms. "You're so fucking beautiful in the morning."

"Stop talking." Her hands slid down the sides of his body. "And kiss me."

"With pleasure."

Konner knew he'd never get enough of this woman. She was absolutely delicious, and the way her body responded under his was even better.

Soon, kissing wasn't enough, and Dakota's grip on his ass urged him for more.

She sighed as he slid into her wet heat.

They made love lazily, taking their time to enjoy every bit of each other after their time apart.

Afterward, he held her in his arms.

"I like this," she said. "I missed you."

"You did?" He brushed her hair away and kissed the nape of her neck. "How much?"

"Probably not as much as you missed me."

"I know that's true." He chuckled. "I did not like being away from you, kitten."

"It's kind of crazy to think that two weeks ago, I didn't know you even existed and now…" She flipped over so she faced him. "I can't imagine being without you."

Konner lifted her hand and pressed her fingers to his lips. "You'll never have to, Dakota. I'm not going anywhere."

She grinned and her eyes flashed with mischief.

"You don't believe me?"

"Oh," she said. "I believe you. But I was just thinking…"

"Uh oh," he teased, and she tried to wriggle free from his grasp. "What exactly was your beautiful brain thinking of?"

"You said you're not going to go anywhere, but maybe I could change your mind about that? I mean, I wasn't really planning on Knox, or really, having a brother at all. But now that he's here…"

In a flash, his bear was on alert.

Knox.

Once he'd managed to pull his bear under control the night before, it was easy to see that Knox was in fact Dakota's brother. The family resemblance was uncanny. And although Konner would have been happier with some sort of DNA test to prove it, even if he did demand it, it wasn't likely to happen in any kind of timely fashion in a place like Predator Peak.

At ay rate, it would be an unnecessary step. Dakota's instincts told her exactly who Knox was. And when it came to shifters, instincts were often more reliable than blood tests anyway. Whether Konner liked it or not, Knox was her brother.

It wasn't that Konner didn't like him. He didn't *know* him.

He did, however, think it was suspicious that it was only once Konner was out of town and Dakota was on her own that her long-lost brother she'd never heard of decided to make himself known after sending her cryptic messages. Very suspicious.

And Konner had to keep his guard up. Especially when it came to Dakota. He wouldn't put it past King to take other measures to find his daughter. Sure, Konner was fairly confident that the man had bought his story about Angelica disappearing, presumed dead. *But what if he hadn't?*

What if he'd already found her on his own and he'd recruited her biological brother to bring her back? Could they trust Knox? It was too early to tell.

"Konner? Hello?"

He blinked hard, refocusing on his mate. "Sorry," he said. "I was just thinking about something."

Dakota gave him a look that told him that she knew exactly what he was thinking about. Konner had no doubt that she could sense his reluctance through their bond when it came to her *brother*.

"You were saying something about Knox?" He tried his best to sound casual. "What about him?"

For a moment, she looked as if she were going to call him out. Instead, she simply shook her head. "I was also talking about convincing you to go somewhere—"

"No." He put a stop to that line of conversation. "There is no way I'm leaving—"

"I didn't say anything about you leaving me." She laughed and slipped from the bed.

Konner immediately missed the warmth of her body next to him, but the sight of her nakedness on full display for him was an adequate consolation.

She flicked her hair back from her face and looked over her shoulder at him. "I was thinking that maybe we could *all* go somewhere. As a—"

"Do not say *family*." He rolled his eyes and tried not to groan out loud.

Her laughter filled the room. "I was going to say that maybe we could all go somewhere as a *group*." She shook her head. "It might be a little early to start using the word family, don't you think?"

"I do." Konner sat up against the headboard. "But...never mind." He ran his hands back through his hair. "Where exactly were you thinking we should *all* go?"

She'd woken up with the idea to take a trip to Quartz Lake, and she was glad she had. It was the perfect way for all of them to get to know each other a little better as a *group*. Not quite a family. Not yet anyway.

Dakota snuck a glance at Konner, who was unloading the supplies for a day at the lake out of the back of his truck. He'd been adamant about not using the word family. Not that she was going to. At least not yet, but... She let her gaze travel around the little group. Knox was setting up a picnic spot, putting out chairs and doing his best to stay out of Konner's way. Ivy and Nolan had just arrived with Jager and Ruby, who was already running around the beach with an inflatable unicorn around her waist.

It was an odd group to call *family*. But that's exactly what it was—or could be. She'd been surrounded by people her whole life. Tutors and nannies, of course. There was Aunt Michelle, and a few others, but they always kept their distance, as if they'd been warned away from her. And then there was the steady stream of *business associates* of her father's. But despite all the people, Dakota always felt alone. And she certainly never felt like she had *family*.

Her eyes landed on Knox.

Her brother.

There was so much more she wanted to know about their mother. *What was her favorite food? Did she talk to herself when she thought no one was watching? What about music? Did she sing in the shower? Or in the car? What did her voice sound like?*

"This is nice." Ivy appeared at her side, pulling her from her thoughts. "It's been ages since I've had a lake day, and the weather is perfect."

Dakota looked up at the blue sky. It was already such a beautiful day, without a cloud in the sky. "I've never had a lake day," she told Ivy.

"Never?"

She shook her head. "It wasn't really a thing you did in the city." Reflexively, she clamped her lips shut, afraid of saying too much, but she was among family now. She was safe. "And my dad wasn't really the type of dad who did things like that." She pointed to where Jager was already sitting on the sand, legs spread wide with a pile of buckets and various tools next to him that he was using to help Ruby build a sandcastle.

Ivy laughed. "He is a pretty awesome dad." She gave Dakota a warm smile. "I know I told you that your past doesn't matter to me, Dakota. But if you ever want to talk about it, I just want you to know that I'd be happy to listen."

"I appreciate that." She returned her friend's smile. "And I will probably take you up on that. But today is all about having fun and bringing everyone together."

"Ah." Ivy nodded. "I see. That's what this is all about." She turned slowly and took in the group. Konner was by the firepit, trying to start a fire while Knox stood by and watched. His arms were crossed over his chest, and he wore a knowing smirk as Konner struggled with the kindling and the matches. "You're trying to get them to like each other."

Dakota spun to face her friend. "Do you think they hate each other?"

Ivy raised an eyebrow. "Hmm, a brand-new mate *and* a brand-new brother? I think there's a whole lot of alpha male shit going on there." She waved in the direction of the men in question where Knox was now crouching down next to Konner and trying to offer assistance in lighting the fire. Even from where they stood, Dakota could see the firm set of Konner's jaw as he continued to struggle with creating a spark.

"Hopefully today will help." She sighed. "I mean, I hope it doesn't hurt."

"It will be fine." Ivy nudged her gently in the ribs. "But you might not want to let those two go into the water unattended if you want them both to come back." She chuckled and took

Dakota's hand. "Come on. Let's go stick our feet in the lake until we can't feel our toes."

———

"This is nice."

Konner dipped his paddle in the water and pulled back hard, propelling the canoe out into the lake, farther away from the beach and Knox.

He'd had just about enough of the new guy. The irony that, up until only a few days ago, *he* had been the new guy was not lost on him. But that was different. Konner was Dakota's mate. *Fated mate.* Knox was her half-brother. It was very different. And even if it wasn't, Konner didn't care. Knox was getting on his last nerve, and the last thing he wanted to do was let his bear loose at the beach. Dakota would be pissed.

"Are you having a nice day?"

Her smile was the only answer he needed, and it was an excellent reminder what was important. Dakota. She was the only thing that was important. And if her mangey cat of a brother made her happy, then he'd just have to learn to deal with it.

"I know this is all happening so fast." She leaned forward a bit. "All of it." She waved an arm in the air, and Konner couldn't help but chuckle.

Fast?

Light speed was more like it.

"But you know what's weird?"

He shook his head.

"I'm not freaked out by it." She dropped her head to one side and her long hair fell like a silk curtain over her shoulder. "I mean, I should be. Especially considering…" She took a deep breath and exhaled slowly before starting over. "Especially considering where I come from."

Konner worked to keep his face neutral. He focused on dipping the paddles in as smoothly as possible, gliding them over the smooth surface of the water. "I hate that your father was so awful to you." Konner gritted his teeth. "You didn't deserve to grow up like that, kitten. And I'll do my—"

"I like it when you call me that." Her lips curled up into a small smile, and warmth rushed through him.

If she liked it, he would never stop.

A moment later, the smile slid off her face again, and Konner knew there was more she needed to say. "What's got you all twisted up, kitten? What are you thinking about?"

She sighed and looked up at the cloudless sky. "My father," she began. "I told you he was a cruel man."

"That's a generous description," he mumbled, but she heard him. Konner swallowed hard and inhaled deeply as he set the paddle across the canoe, giving her his full attention.

"You've heard of him then?"

Konner nodded once.

Dakota accepted his response. "I don't think he ever recovered from my mother leaving." She stared out at the lake for a moment. "She spent her life hiding, Konner."

"She must have thought it was the only way."

"She must have." She shook her head. "But maybe there was another way. Maybe *I* had another way instead of running from my father and Dominic."

There was no hope to control the growl that rumbled from his chest at the mention of the panther shifter.

Dakota tipped her head in acknowledgment of his possessiveness but continued to speak. "My father doesn't like to lose. And Dominic...he's the heir to one of the most powerful Mafia families in North America."

He knew that already.

"He makes my father look like a pussycat, Konner. Dominic won't give up looking for me either."

Unless you're dead.

Konner swallowed hard. He couldn't tell her that they would, in fact, stop looking for her because as far as they knew, she was dead.

He tipped his head up to the sky and took a moment to pull himself together. Maybe he should just tell her the truth. He could tell her what he'd done and why he knew for a fact that she was safe.

"But I can't hide anymore, Konner."

His head snapped back, and he stared at her. "What do you mean?"

"Don't you see? Knox found me. They'll be able to find me, too." She shook her head slowly. "I can't keep hiding. I won't."

She *had* to keep hiding. He'd just told King she was dead. If she waltzed back into town now, she'd not only put herself at an unimaginable risk, King would kill him. And his family.

"You don't think Knox will sell you out?" He'd kill him. Konner's gaze swept the shoreline and landed on the cat. He'd kill him right now to keep that from happening.

"No." When Konner didn't react, Dakota said it again, "No, Konner. Knox wouldn't say anything."

"You know that?" he challenged her. "Do you trust him with your life?"

Some of the fight went out of her, and she slumped in her seat. "I don't *know* it. But I have to believe it."

A tear slipped down her cheek.

Fuck.

Konner tucked the paddle inside the boat and as carefully as he could, without rocking the boat, he moved toward her and took her hands in his.

"I don't want to spend my life hiding," she admitted. "I deserve more than that. *We* deserve more."

"I'll keep you safe, Dakota." He pulled her into his arms.

The canoe rocked gently as he kissed her. "No matter what. But I don't think you need to do anything where your father is concerned."

"Really?" She pulled back. "You don't?"

"No." He shook his head and cursed himself inwardly for not telling her the truth. Maybe he was making a mistake by not coming clean right now. But he didn't think so. Everything he'd done had been about keeping her safe and getting King to leave her alone once and for all. He needed to follow through with that plan. It was the only way they would be free.

King needed to believe that Angelica was dead. If he told Dakota the truth now, it would jeopardize everything. He hated keeping any kind of secret from her, but it was only for a little bit longer. He'd tell her the truth when he knew she was safe for good. "If he wanted to find you, he would have by now." He swallowed hard against the lie. "Knox only found you because he had information your father didn't. And he got lucky, frankly. Besides, if he does try anything, I'll keep you safe, Dakota." He stared deeply into her eyes, willing her to believe him and to trust him.

"Plus, I think despite the fact that you clearly doubt yourself, you've demonstrated on more than one occasion that you are, in fact, perfectly capable of looking after yourself." He wiggled his eyebrow and touched his now perfectly healed cheek to make his point. "My mate is a strong, feisty cougar." He risked rocking the boat and pulled her down so she lay on the bottom of the canoe before he moved overtop her.

"What else is your mate?" Her eyelids fluttered, and she ran a finger down his chest to the waistband of his shorts.

The way it always did, his body reacted to her touch with an all-consuming need.

"Ohh...." Konner pushed the fabric of her tiny bikini down, off her perfect breasts, and pressed kisses on each of her pert nipples. "My mate is sexy as hell," he said when her back arched up against him. "She's smart." He kissed her flat stomach, letting his tongue dip into her belly button until she squealed. "She's just mysterious enough to keep me guessing." His hand slipped beneath the band of her shorts, and past her bikini bottoms to find her hot, wet core. "And she drives me fucking crazy." Konner slipped a finger inside her heat.

Dakota groaned in response. Her eyes were closed, her head tipped back as she gave herself over to him completely. She was both vulnerable and fiercely sexy.

It didn't take long before she was moaning in need as Konner teased a climax from her. As she came undone and let herself go with only the touch of his fingers, Konner felt nothing but love and a deep connection to her. His mate. She cried out her release and it echoed across the water, and Konner knew without a doubt that there was nothing he wouldn't do to keep her safe and protected.

Even if that meant lying to her. For just a little bit longer.

Chapter Fourteen

IT HAD BEEN ALMOST a week since their day at the lake, and as far as Dakota was concerned, her plan to force them all together had worked. Although Konner and Knox still weren't best friends, they no longer looked as if they were going to tear each other apart.

Well, at least not most of the time.

Upon Dakota's insistence, Knox had moved out of the cabin behind the bar and was now staying in her guest room. She could tell that Konner wasn't thrilled with the idea, but so far, he hadn't objected, which was good, because he couldn't live in a short-term rental forever, and Dakota planned to ask him to officially move in with her, too. It only made sense considering they spent all their time together already. And Dakota didn't see that changing anytime soon. They couldn't get enough of each other.

She couldn't remember a time in her life when she'd ever been as happy. The three of them were starting to fall into a bit of a routine. Dakota would spend her mornings with Konner, making love, drinking coffee, and sometimes making love again before finally spending a few hours on her business. She knew she was probably rushing through her content creation, but her followers hadn't complained and more than a few of them had commented on the new sparkle in her eyes.

In the afternoons, she'd go out with Knox, leaving Konner to work on his book in peace. Growing up in the prairies, Knox was obsessed with the mountains. Together they explored the woods. Sometimes they would shift and let their cougars run. But Dakota preferred to hike because that way they could talk and catch up on all the years they'd missed out on.

In the evenings, the three of them would join Nolan and Ivy, and sometimes Jager and Ruby, for dinner. Now that Ivy was starting to get to the uncomfortable phase of her pregnancy, they usually gathered at their house, where she could be the most comfortable.

"I swear." Ivy sank back into the couch. "This baby is going to be a monster. I don't know how I'm going to make it, Dakota."

"You're going to make it." Dakota shook her head from where she stood at the kitchen counter, tossing a salad. The men were all in the yard, grilling steak. "And you're going to have the sweetest, healthiest baby ever. I can't wait to meet her."

"I still think it would be pretty cool if you and Konner had a—"

Dakota held up a hand to stop her friend. She'd decided years ago that she didn't want to bring children into the world. With no real example of a loving family, she didn't feel equipped to be a mother. Maybe that would change one day, but not any time soon.

"All I'm saying is…" Ivy struggled to adjust herself on the couch. "Never say never."

"I didn't say never."

"I think those were your exact words." Ivy laughed. "But that was before."

"Before?"

"Before Konner." Her friend grinned. "Everything is different when your mate comes along, right?"

Dakota shook her head and refocused on the salad, but she was laughing because Ivy was right. Everything *was* different. "Okay," she relented.

"Okay?" Ivy struggled to sit up.

"Don't get excited. I'm not saying that I'm going to have babies. I'm just saying that I won't discard the idea completely."

"That sounds like a win to me."

"Who's winning?" Knox walked into the kitchen and the conversation and looked between the two women with a grin on his face.

"I'll be winning," Ivy said. "If you can help me off of this couch."

Dakota laughed while Knox went to help. "You just sat down."

"And now I need to pee." With a heave, Knox had her on her feet in a flash. "Again," she added with a groan. "I'll be back."

As soon as her friend was gone, Dakota slid the salad bowl toward her brother. "If you can grab this, I'll—"

Her phone rang in her pocket, and she froze. She almost never got calls, which meant that maybe the message she'd sent as discreetly as she could to her Aunt Michelle had been received.

"I'll meet you outside." Dakota did her best to sound calm when she was feeling anything but on the inside. If Knox noticed, he didn't say anything. She pulled her phone out of her pocket and slipped out the door to the front porch for some privacy as she answered the call.

"Angelica? Is that really you?"

"So how's it all going?" Nolan handed Konner a bottle of beer.

They'd been left in charge of the grill while Ivy and Dakota put together the salad and Knox...well, who the hell knew what Knox was doing. Konner was just glad to get a few minutes of respite without the man hanging over his shoulder.

There was clearly some alpha male possessiveness going on between them as each of them tried to lay *claim* in some way to Dakota. It was stupid, and Konner knew it, but it wasn't likely to go away anytime soon.

"It's all..." Konner twisted the cap off his bottle and contemplated the beer for a moment before shaking his head slightly and tipping it to his lips.

"That good, huh?" Nolan laughed.

"It's not that it's bad." Konner wiped his mouth with the back of his hand. "Things with Dakota are...damn. They're great." He smiled the way he always did when he thought of his mate.

"Fated mates are like that." Nolan nodded in understanding. "So damn great."

"And frustrating as hell."

Nolan almost spat out his beer. "I don't think that's a fated mate thing so much as a female thing." He glanced over his shoulder. "Do *not* tell Ivy I said that."

"I do not have a death wish." Konner took another pull on his beer.

"Seriously, though." Nolan turned stoic again. "I know it's a lot to have a new mate and then with Knox...it's got to be kind of intense."

Never mind the whole *keeping his mate's father from finding her and killing them both.* Oh yeah, Nolan had *no* idea. It had been a long time since Konner had a buddy he could confide in. His sister had always been there of course, but it was different with

Cressa. Probably because she was younger and for as long as Konner could remember, he'd been working to protect her and keep her safe. The last thing he ever wanted to do was worry her with the truth.

"You know what?" He dropped his head for a moment. "It *has* been intense. It's not that I don't like Knox." Now he was lying. "It's just that…"

"You want to be alone with Dakota?"

Konner laughed and used his beer bottle to point at his friend. "Exactly. I mean, we're newly mated. We should be holed up somewhere, fucking like…well, like new mates."

"I agree, man. There is no way I would have been sharing a house with Ivy's brother in those early days." He let out a low whistle. "I'm pretty sure Jager would have murdered me if he'd been privy to some of the things we…well, it doesn't matter."

A flare of jealousy shot through Konner. He'd heard about how he and Ivy had holed up at the hunting cabin for weeks, concreting their bond by basically having sex twenty-four hours a day. He knew it was different for wolves, but it wasn't *that* different. And the idea of being able to walk around the house naked so he could take every opportunity to consummate their relationship was very, *very* appealing.

"You know, you could always use the hunting cabin for a bit if you wanted to?" Nolan had moved to the grill and flipped the steaks. "I'm going to start some renovation up there, but not until after the baby is born. If you want to get away, just let me know."

Konner glanced toward the house where Knox had disappeared inside to see whether the women needed any help. "It's tempting."

It was *very* tempting. Unfortunately, he had something else he needed to take care of first.

"There actually is something I was hoping you could help me out with, though."

Nolan looked over his shoulder. "Whatever you need," he said easily. "You're family now. Part of the pack."

Never in his life did he think he'd be part of a *pack*. Then again, he never expected a wolf to be one of his closest friends. "I really appreciate you saying that, man. I feel the same way."

"So, what do you need?"

Konner swallowed hard. He'd thought of a dozen different scenarios, and if there'd been any other way, he would have taken it. Never in his life had he done what he was about to do, and he'd always sworn he wouldn't. But ultimately, he couldn't think of any other way to keep those he loved safe. "I know this is a big ask," Konner started with a sigh. "And I wouldn't ask if it wasn't really important, but—"

"Whatever it is," Nolan stopped him, "the answer is yes. I told you...you're pack. I've got you."

Konner exhaled slowly and looked down. "I can't believe I'm asking you for this, but is there any way I can borrow ten thousand dollars? I'll pay you back as soon as I can. With interest."

"Of course."

"I wouldn't ask if it wasn't—wait. What?"

"I said yes." Nolan nodded.

"But you didn't even think about it, and it's a lot of money, and—"

"Of course I'll help you out. Is that it?"

Konner nodded, a little stunned. Over the years, he'd slowly sold everything he could, which wasn't much since his father had already hocked anything of real value to feed his gambling addiction. He'd cashed out the small education savings account his mom had squirreled away for him, and then he'd worked off the rest of his father's five-hundred-thou-sand-dollar debt. Ten thousand seemed like such a small amount in the grand scheme of things, but it was all that was left before he, and his family, were free. And with no other way to get the money...grateful didn't even begin to sum up how Konner felt.

"I can't tell you what this means to me, Nolan."

"Don't worry about it." He waved his hand. "I know you wouldn't ask if it wasn't important."

"So important." He drained the rest of his beer. "If you wouldn't mind not mentioning anything to Dakota about it, I'd really appreciate it. I have a few things I need to take care of before I let her in on it all." And he would tell her everything. But first, he needed to take care of King and make sure she was safe. That was the most important thing.

The last few days had made that crystal clear. King was growing impatient with his absence. He wanted Konner back in the city for a full debriefing. Konner couldn't put it off anymore. First, he needed to make sure King believed Angelica was dead; he'd pay his way out of his debt to ensure his mother and sister's safety, and then he'd return home to Dakota and finally start their life together, free of secrets.

"No problem."

"I actually have to go to the city for a few days and take care of some things," he told Nolan. "But maybe when I get back, it would be good for Dakota and me to go up to the hunting cabin and get that alone time."

"Anytime, man." Nolan flipped the steaks onto a platter. "What's going on in the city?"

"Who's going to the city?" Knox chose that moment to rejoin them in the backyard, a big bowl of salad in his hands. He set it on the picnic table and helped himself to a beer. "You?" He pointed at Konner, who bit back a rude reply.

He really did need to try harder to get along with the guy. For Dakota's sake.

"I've got a few things to take care of with the lease on my place." The lie slipped easily off his tongue. "Doesn't look like

I'll be going back there for a while." He smiled, but Knox didn't return it. "Where are the girls?"

Knox stared at him a moment longer before answering. "Ivy had to use the restroom."

"Again?" Nolan chuckled and shook his head. "I swear, that baby is going to test her mama's last nerve before she's even born."

"And Dakota had to take a call." Knox gestured toward the front yard. "It sounded important."

"Important?" Immediately Konner's bear was alert. *What kind of important call did Dakota get?*

Aware that the others' eyes were on him, he forced himself to stay calm.

Fuck.

The sooner he was done with King, the better.

The familiar voice came over the line and for a moment, Dakota couldn't speak.

"Angelica?"

She inhaled deeply before answering in a shaky voice. "It's me."

"How are... Where... Oh my. I thought you were dead."

Dead?

"I'm fine. Not dead."

Definitely not dead, and she was better than fine. But Dakota didn't think that the details of her situation were a priority at the moment. When she'd sent the message from a fake account on social media, she hadn't been entirely sure what she would say to her aunt if she did reach out. Truthfully, Dakota hadn't really expected it to work.

She'd set up a temporary online phone number that would route the call to her cell phone just in case Michelle couldn't be trusted. Her gut told her that she could, especially after hearing how she'd helped her mother so long ago. Still, a little caution wasn't a bad idea.

"I'm glad you called." She straightened her shoulders and took a breath.

"Of course I called. I was so worried when you left. I thought maybe…well, it didn't matter what I thought. I'm just glad you're okay now."

"I am. And I wasn't trying to worry anyone." Dakota shook her head. "It didn't occur to me that anyone *would* worry."

Her aunt was quiet for a moment. "Angelica, I know I failed you."

"You did—"

"I did. I promised your mother I would watch out for you." Michelle's voice was thick with emotion. "It might not seem like it, but I tried my best. I really did. My brother…your father…he's not a kind man."

That was an understatement.

"But it wasn't until you grew up and became of age that I started to worry about you. I could see what Javier had planned for you. I tried to talk him out of it, but he couldn't be swayed. I never should have let it get as far as it did. I should have—"

"It doesn't matter now. I'm safe."

"And I'm glad of it," Michelle said. "I should have helped you get free years ago, but I'm glad you had the strength that I didn't. You're a brave girl. You've always been so much stronger than you ever knew. I'm so pleased you finally realized it."

Dakota let a little smile cross her lips. There were times when she certainly didn't feel it, but more and more she was starting to believe it. "But wait." Something Michelle said a moment ago resonated. "You thought I was dead?"

"Of course I did. Everyone does."

A strange mixture of sadness and excitement washed through her. If her father thought she was dead, he'd stop looking for her. But at the same time, it was strange to celebrate your own *death*.

"But, why?" Suddenly exhausted, Dakota sat on the wooden bench Ivy had on the porch. "Why would they think that?"

"As you can imagine, Angelica, when you disappeared, your father was enraged. And Dominic…" There was a long pause before she continued. "It wasn't good. Dominic demanded that Javier find you at once. He sent men after you, of course, but when he couldn't immediately find traces of you, he had to call most of his men back."

Most.

"I don't know who it was, but he did have one man dedicated to finding you. And from what I understand, he got quite close. Reports started coming in that he thought he'd located you but was keeping his distance for a bit just to be sure."

She was glad she was sitting down because the more Michelle spoke, the less Dakota could feel her hands and feet. An icy fear began to spread through her veins, making it hard to think.

"Someone was following me?"

Keeping his distance.

"That's how I understand it," Michelle continued. "Remember, I wasn't privy to all the information. I did my best to inquire, of course, and I listened where I could. I know the reports that were coming in were promising enough that wedding plans had once again started up. Dominic flew in and was impatient to secure the marriage."

Dakota had to ask the question, but she had to. "How long ago was that?"

"Hmmm… My memory isn't quite what it used to be."

Dakota tried not to rush her as she did the math in her own

head. She'd been with Konner for about a month, but she'd felt him following her for weeks before that. *But what about Knox?* He'd been watching her, too. *What if...*

"At least a month and a half ago, maybe two months when the first reports came in," Michelle finally said. "But it could have been a few weeks on either end—I just didn't hear about it."

A month? Weeks?

Had Konner been hired to follow her? Was he working for her father? Was Knox?

No. It couldn't be possible. Konner was her fated mate. He would never...but he *had* admitted to following her.

No. She refused to believe it. But what was the other option? *Knox? Her brother?*

He'd also admitted to finding her and watching her before reaching out.

Dakota's mind spun with the possibilities. None of them good.

"And now they think I'm dead?" She forced herself to focus on what was important. "But how?"

"Javier's man tracked you to Alaska," she said. "There was evidence that you fell prey to a serial killer who's known to the area."

"And they accepted that?"

"Your father did."

She didn't say anything about him grieving her loss, not that Dakota expected it, but still, it would have been nice.

"I think he was relieved to be done with it all. I assume they must be working out a new deal of sorts. Once I heard of your death, well, I kind of kept my distance, Angelica. There was no more reason to..."

"I understand." It wasn't a replacement for a lifetime of feeling alone and not having anyone looking out for her. But it helped a little bit to know that at least someone in her family cared enough to listen for news of her. Even if she hadn't done anything to help.

"To know that you're safe, Angelica...it's the greatest gift."

Safe.

The voices from the backyard drifted out to reach her ears. *Knox. Konner.* Was *she safe?*

She no longer knew.

Dakota blew out a breath. There was only one way to ensure her safety. "And you won't say anything now that you know I'm alive?"

"Of course not."

Dakota wanted to believe her aunt, but trust wasn't easily earned.

And she was very quickly learning that there may not be anyone she could trust except herself.

Chapter Fifteen

THE REST of the dinner party the night before had been awkward and strained, but Konner was aware that it might just have been his own preoccupation with his secrets. Dakota seemed distant when she rejoined them, but he hadn't been able to get her alone to ask her about it. And when they got home, she'd gone straight to bed, claiming a headache.

The sooner they could put all this behind them and he could be open and honest with her once and for all, the better. And it was all going to be over soon. Yes, he was trading one debt for another, but with Nolan, Konner knew that lending him the money didn't come with any strings. It was a very different type of debt and one that Konner planned to pay back as quickly as he could. Even though his family wouldn't be at risk any longer, he was more than ready to start fresh and, for the first time in his life, not owe anyone anything.

Konner still couldn't believe that Nolan had agreed so readily to help him out with the rest of the money he owed to King. And without any explanation. All because he was *pack*.

As a bear shifter, Konner had never been part of a pack before. Obviously.

He hadn't ever had anything even remotely close to the friendships he was already starting to build in Predator Peak in such a short time. Growing up, he'd always been ashamed of his father and his home life. Having people over was out of the question most of the time. And on the few occasions he'd dared to bring someone home, inevitably it ended in disaster when his father came home drunk, or angry because he'd lost at the casino—again. It wasn't worth the risk.

When the other kids stopped inviting Konner over to their houses, it was just easier to remain a loner. And once he got old enough to get a job and start putting food on the table, that's where all his extra time went until, finally, he could drop out of school altogether and work directly for King to chip away at the debt that had, even back then, been gargantuan.

Konner's teachers had tried to intervene and keep him in school, especially his English teacher, who was sure he could earn a scholarship to college. "It's exceptionally rare to find talent like yours, Konner. You could write the next great novel. But you have to finish high school at the very least."

"I can still write the next great novel," he'd told her. "But staying in school isn't an option. My family needs me." A few years later, his dad was dead, and that statement had never been more true.

He still planned to finish that first novel, but just as it was back then, Konner's priority was his family. Only now, that family had expanded to include Dakota, too. Which that meant that now, more than ever, it was crucial to take care of this debt and get rid of King once and for all.

He planned to leave for the coast at first light, but when he'd woken, Dakota was already gone. He showered, changed, and packed a small bag before heading down to the kitchen. He didn't plan to be gone long. It shouldn't take more than a few minutes to get King out of his life for good. But he wasn't a fool, either.

Once the debt was paid, King wouldn't have a hold on him. But that didn't mean that he wouldn't torment Cressa and his mother. Konner had been around long enough to know that there was no way you could escape the grip of the family and not leave town. Even then, the farther, the better. It would very much be an out of sight, out of mind situation. And that meant his mother and sister were going to have to come back to Predator Peak with him, at least for a little while.

He didn't know how he was going to work out all the logistics yet. Especially without a job and a still unfinished manuscript. But he'd worry about those details later.

First, he needed to find his mate, who wasn't to be found in the kitchen either. Instead, her obnoxious brother sat at the table, drinking a cup of coffee.

"Morning." He could still try to be civil to the man. After all, it wasn't his fault that his timing was horrible. *Oh, wait. It was.* He'd already been out of Dakota's life for so long; would it really have mattered if he'd waited another few months, or even a year before reappearing?

Knox didn't bother looking up from his coffee and offered little more than a grunt in return.

"Any idea where your sister is?"

"Shouldn't you know?" He tilted his head and narrowed his eyes in Konner's direction. "Aren't you supposed to be connected or something?"

"Yeah, that's not really how it works." Truth be told, Konner still hadn't worked out all the details of having a mate. Especially considering he'd been actively keeping part of himself closed off from her, and that was only because it was necessary for her protection. But that would be over soon, too. As soon as he took care of these last few details, he'd be able to let her in fully and completely, and their bond would be stronger than ever. "It's not like I have a tracker on her or something."

"Huh." Knox gave him a half-shrug. "I thought that's exactly what it was like. But I certainly don't know."

"No," Konner snapped. "You don't." He grabbed a mug from the cupboard, but when he lifted the coffeepot, it was empty. "Did you finish the coffee and— What's this?" His attention was drawn to a note taped on the fridge.

"It's not my job to make sure you—"

"Shut up." Konner grabbed the note that was addressed to both of them and opened the folded paper, his stomach already twisted in a knot. "There's a note."

Knox shoved back his chair and joined him, reading over his shoulder.

Konner and Knox,
There's something I need to take care of.

Konner's bear was on alert as he continued to read.

I can't trust either of you. I'm going alone.

"What the fuck does that mean?" Knox grabbed the note from him. "Why can't she trust us? I'm her fucking brother, and you…"

"I lied to her." The realization hit him hard. She must have discovered the truth, and now…

Knox spun on him. "What do you mean, you lied to her?"

"You won't understand." The last fucking thing he wanted

to do was get into some macho alpha fight with this asshole. "There's no—"

Knox's eyes flashed gold, his razor-sharp teeth slipping out between his lips. "Try me."

Konner's bear growled, ready to rip the cat apart, but that wasn't going to solve anything. "I was going to tell her everything, as soon as I dealt with it," he started to explain, left with no other choice. "I was going to see her father today and—"

"Her father? King? What do you—"

"I worked for him." Konner dodged Knox's swing and held up a hand. "I don't anymore. Or, I won't as soon as I pay him off." Again, Knox lunged for him, but Konner caught him by the shoulders before his punch could connect. "It wasn't my choice, man. He would've taken my mother." He shoved Knox, who snarled and came at him again, harder.

"So, what? You were working for her father, and all of this was a bunch of bullshit?" Knox wiped the hair off his face, before lunging again for Konner.

Konner missed his attack, by an inch; the other man's claws left lines in the drywall where Konner's head had just been. "Enough." Dodging the cat was getting old, quickly. And as much as Konner would like to fight him, it wasn't going to help Dakota. "I didn't know she was my mate. I was told to come get her. And as soon as I realized who she was to me, I knew I could never take her anywhere near him." He moved around the table, putting the furniture between them. "I've been trying to figure out how to keep her safe," he told Knox.

"You lied to her. She's your *mate.*"

"I couldn't tell her the truth. Not until I figured it out. It wasn't safe. She would have—fuck." Realization crashed through him. Ignoring Knox, he lunged for the note that had fluttered to the floor and read it again, this time finishing it.

There's something I need to take care of.
I can't trust either of you. I'm going alone.
I've spent too long hiding.
That ends today.

"What the fuck does that mean?" Knox swiped the note from his hand, and Konner let him.

He took a breath and let it fill his lungs completely as the truth settled over him. "She's going to him," he said aloud. "To King."

"Fuck."

Konner turned to face his mate's brother. "That's something we can both agree on."

Chapter Sixteen

DAKOTA HADN'T BEEN able to sleep. The fact that she'd made it through the rest of the barbecue with everyone before she could claim—as soon as it was reasonable to do so—she had a headache and leave was a miracle. She'd been sure that Ivy would call her out or force her to stay. But her friend, too, was tired, and an early night seemed like a good idea for everyone.

She hadn't been able to stop thinking about what Michelle told her. There'd been someone following her. Her father had sent someone after her. Of course he had. That made sense. She knew her father wasn't the type to give up without some sort of fight. It was everything else that didn't make sense. *Had it been Knox following her? Or Konner?*

And why, if it were either of them, had they not told her the truth?

It hurt to think that she'd been so open with Konner about her family and who she was and still, he'd held back. And Knox. How much did she really know about him? Yes, he was her brother. She knew that with certainty, but did that mean he was loyal to her? He could be working for *the family*.

Her brother and her mate—if she couldn't trust them, then could she really trust anyone?

Maybe she should have confronted both of them and just gotten to the bottom of things. But if one of them was working for her father...she didn't want to believe that was true. And her gut told her it couldn't possibly be true. Yet...

It was hard to ignore what her aunt had said.

She'd tossed and turned all night, trying to decide what to do. Ultimately, Dakota knew there was only one thing she could do. Michelle was right. She *was* strong and brave. There had been too many times in her life when she'd been made to feel weak and insignificant. Her father had kept her down for too long. But the truth was, she was anything but weak. She'd been born to be an alpha, and it was long past time she behaved like one. She couldn't depend on anyone else. This was something she had to do for herself.

It had ripped at her heart to leave without a word in the early hours before dawn. Despite her confusion toward both Konner and Knox and her hurt, they were bonded. There was no denying that. And she would work it out with both of them in time.

She had to believe that.

But it would have to wait because the one thing she was now sure of was that she couldn't move on with her new life until she left her old one behind once and for all.

She'd moved fast through the mountains, ignoring the ache in her chest the farther she got from Konner. She crossed the distance quickly until she got to the familiar neighborhood.

Her childhood home looked the same as it always had. It was a massive heritage home perched on one of Vancouver's most prestige streets. The grounds were protected by a high fence. Dakota skipped the gate at the front of the property and moved to the back of the lot and the hole in the fencing that was covered by thick hedges. She'd discovered the escape route when she was a child and had made good use of it, escaping unnoticed to walk around the community and, when she felt particularly daring, taking public transit to the sea wall to sit with her legs dangling over the ocean.

The gap in the fencing was still there, and Dakota slipped through it, before shifting into her human form and dressing carefully in the clothes she'd brought with her. It had been a risk to move through the city as a cougar, but the thick vegetation in the upper-scale communities gave her plenty of cover and she didn't want to waste any time.

She knew as soon as she stepped out onto the lawn, she'd be spotted. She'd counted on it.

Sure enough, she'd only made it halfway across the grounds, to the patio door by the pool, when security reached her and escorted her into her own home. Correction—it *had* been where she lived, but the grand mansion had never felt like home. Not like the little two-bedroom house she'd bought in Predator Peak.

As she'd expected, she was led directly to her father's office, where he was already waiting for her. It had only been a little over a year since she'd seen him, but Javier King looked as if he'd aged more than ten years.

"Angelica."

There was no emotion in her father's voice as he examined her from behind his massive walnut desk. She used to be scared of that desk. Or was it always just the man who sat behind it? Either way, neither the man nor the desk seemed as large and intimidating as they used to.

If he thought she was dead, he didn't seem surprised at all to see her standing before him now. In fact, just like his voice, his body language gave nothing away.

Dakota straightened her shoulders and looked him straight in the eye. She refused to back down or show any kind of fear. She was not afraid. He couldn't make her do anything she didn't want to do. She was an adult. She didn't need him the way she once thought she did. "Father." Her voice was strong. "I've come to say goodbye."

"Goodbye?" His voice boomed through the room. "But you've only just arrived. Don't you mean to tell me you've come to say hello?"

"No." She inhaled slowly through her nose. "I mean to tell you goodbye now. This time, I will be leaving this house, this family and *you*, Father. I've come to say goodbye." She repeated the words she'd decided upon on her travels west. There was so much she wanted to say. Questions that she deserved answers to. But Dakota knew in her heart there was no point. There was nothing he could say to her now that would make up for an entire lifetime of loneliness, neglect, and being treated like a possession.

"Just like that?"

She nodded and clasped her hands in front of her.

Javier inhaled deeply and tipped his head up to the ceiling. When he leveled his gaze upon her once more, there was the trace of a smile. "Okay."

"Okay?" She tried and no doubt, failed, to not look surprised.

"Okay," he repeated. "After all, you are an adult, and you are capable of your own decisions. I have to respect that."

"You do?"

"Yes, Angelica." His voice held a trace of humor in it. "Please." He gestured toward one of the wingback chairs that sat across from his desk. "I know you've expressed your interest in leaving, but if you could spare a few minutes…after all, up until you walked in here, I feared my only daughter was dead."

She let the breath she was holding slip from her lungs, and some of the anger she'd been holding fell away. *He was going to let her go.* Maybe she'd misread him all along.

"Please," he said again, and the rest of her resolve dissolved. "Sit for a minute."

Maybe she could get those answers she was looking for after all.

"Okay." She nodded and moved toward the chair. "But just for a few minutes."

"Of course." Javier's face softened.

Despite everything and all the history between them, somewhere deep inside her, she was still a little girl desperately searching for her father's approval and love. Maybe that part of her would always be there.

She took the seat across from him and perched on the edge of the chair.

"Thank you," he said when she was settled. "I know what you must think of me, Angelica. But—"

She opened her mouth to object, but he held up a hand to silence her.

"Don't bother with your objections. I didn't get to be where I am in life without picking up on a few things along the way."

She sat back in the chair.

"There was never a lot of love lost between us, was there, daughter?"

Dakota didn't bother to answer, and something in his tone shifted when he spoke again.

"You were always a little bit too much like your mother."

There was an unmistakable edge to his voice now. Dakota's spine stiffened. "I wouldn't know."

"No." He laughed, but there was no humor in the sound. "You wouldn't, would you?"

And just like that, the hair on the back of her neck stood up.

She should have known better. Dakota closed her eyes and sucked in a breath. There wasn't going to be an opportunity to get answers or to have any kind of real conversation with her father. She shook her head and moved to leave, but his voice, sharp with command, stopped her.

"Sit."

With impeccable timing, the double doors to his office flung open and the man she recognized as Sam entered, as if Javier had been expecting him. She watched as he bent and whispered something in his ear. Javier nodded, never taking his eyes off her.

As his lackey stood and walked away, he sneered in Dakota's direction. She kept her focus on her father, whose lips had curled up into a knowing grin that sent a shot of icy fear through her veins.

She was an idiot. She'd let her guard down and now it was too late.

Dakota jumped up from her chair, but a firm hand pressed her back down a second later.

"You're not thinking of leaving yet, are you?" Javier's fingers tapped methodically on the smooth wooden desk. "From what I understand, things are just about to get interesting."

He gestured with his eyes, but before Dakota could follow his gaze, the door opened once more.

This time, she froze, and the ever-present ache in her chest flared to life with a sharp pain.

Konner.

Fuck.

The moment Konner realized what Dakota had done—what terrible, foolish, reckless thing she'd done—he'd completely ceased to think straight. Or really, at all.

His bear was completely in control as he tore out of the house and headed west, grabbing his already packed bag as he went. His clothing ripped to shreds as he burst out of his skin, shifting into his bear before he even hit the ground.

He'd already been running for about thirty minutes when he finally realized there was a cougar pacing him.

Knox.

He shouldn't have been surprised. And really, if Dakota was in trouble, he would welcome all the help he could get. If Knox was on his side and not working for King. He had to believe he wasn't.

He didn't have a lot of choices.

The most important thing was to get Dakota back. It was all he could think of.

Which was why, when even after he entered the city limits, he didn't bother to shift back to human form. Konner didn't even slow down until he was at the gates to King's compound.

"Now what?" Knox came to stand at his side. With his hands on his hips, he was working to control his breath.

Konner dressed quickly and threw Knox some spare clothes from his bag.

They'd run nonstop for hours to make it into Vancouver as quickly as they did. Konner just hoped it wasn't already too late. He had no idea how much of a head start Dakota had on them.

"You do have a plan, don't you?"

"Of course I do." Konner moved around the side of the yard, away from where he knew the cameras were. "We're going to get her back."

"That's not much of a plan."

Konner whirled on Knox. "You have a better one?"

Knox held his hands up, and for the first time, Konner could see fear in the other man's eyes. "We're going to get her back, man."

He took a breath and exhaled slowly. "She can't be too far ahead of us. There's a good chance she's already in King's office." He pointed in the general direction. "First floor, the window to the left of the patio doors. You go that way." He nodded toward Knox, who acknowledged him with a salute and took off running in the opposite direction.

Konner blew out a breath, shook his head, and muttered to himself, "Beyond that, I don't have a plan at all."

"No shit."

Konner froze. It was a familiar voice, but it wasn't Knox. *Fuck.*

Chapter Seventeen

KONNER.

What the hell was Konner doing there? She hadn't told him where she was going. How could he—*oh.*

Her heart clenched as she realized that it *had* been Konner, her mate, who'd been working for her father. This whole time, while she'd been falling in love with him, telling him all her secrets, and giving him her heart, he'd been working for the enemy.

Her stomach heaved.

No.

It couldn't be him.

But even with the evidence right in front of her, there was something else. The warm heat in her chest where the bond was. It was still there.

Dakota tried not to react to the sight of her mate as he was shoved into the room.

"Konner Stark."

Dakota swung her gaze back to her father, who grinned as if he'd just captured juicy prey.

"I believe I expected you quite some time ago," Javier

continued. "But I must say, your timing is proving to be most interesting."

Dakota looked between them, trying to sort out what was happening. Konner obviously worked for her father, but there was something else. Something more. *But what?*

Her eyes landed on Konner, who held himself incredibly still. His fists were clenched at his sides, but she could see he was working hard not to look defensive.

He didn't turn in her direction, but there was a squeezing sensation in her chest and even through the pain, Dakota could somehow feel him. *Was it the bond? He was reaching out to her. Trying to tell her something.*

But what? And why should she even listen? He'd betrayed her.

"Why don't you start by explaining to me how it's come to be that Angelica is *not* in fact dead the way you told me she was."

What? It was Konner?

Her father turned in her direction again. "You see, dear daughter, up until very recently, I was mourning your loss because the man I'd hired to find you and bring you back to me informed me that you'd disappeared and were presumed dead."

Again, her chest contracted as the bond flared between them. Dakota looked to Konner, but he still wouldn't turn.

She was very quickly putting the pieces together. Konner worked for her father. He'd obviously been tasked with finding her—which he did. And bringing her back—which he did not. Instead, he'd reported that she was dead. Which was what Aunt Michelle told her.

"That doesn't make sense." She tried her best to put on a strong facade of bravado. "Why would he tell you that?"

"Ahh." Javier extended a long finger toward her. "Excellent question, Angelica. Why would a mangy nobody bear shifter risk everything by betraying *me?* The one man who has given him a chance instead of wiping out the rest of his worthless family the way I should have years ago?"

Her chest pulsed as the bond between her and Konner grew stronger. She could see the twitch of his jaw muscle as he clenched his teeth against her father's words.

"In fact..." Javier swung his finger toward Konner and directed his words toward him. "The way I understood it, this was your last job for me. Your debt was almost paid off."

He was paying off a debt?

More pieces of the puzzle slid into place, and Dakota's mind raced to keep up. He was working for her father, but not by choice. That was the first thing she'd heard that even remotely made sense.

"I have your money." Konner spoke through gritted teeth. "I came to pay off my family's debt."

Once more, Dakota's head swung around to look between the two men.

Javier laughed, a chilling sound. "Tsk, tsk, Stark. I think some would say too little, too late."

"What?" Konner took a step forward, but her father's men were right there to grab him and hold him back.

Dakota reacted, every muscle in her body tensing as she reflexively moved to jump to her mate's aid. Fortunately, she caught herself, but not before Konner's eyes finally flicked in her direction.

"What the fuck are you talking about, King?" Konner refocused on the alpha cat. "We had a deal. If I pay you, the deal is done. I have the—"

"No." Javier shook his head a little. "The deal was to bring Angelica back to me. You failed to do that. And I think I'm very quickly understanding why."

Konner struggled against the confines of the men's arms, but they yanked him back, pulling his shoulders sharply behind him.

She knew exactly why. He hadn't brought her back because he was her mate. He hadn't betrayed her. Not really. Not by choice. The reality of the twisted situation they were in slammed into her.

Dakota swallowed back a gasp at the twist of pain on Konner's face.

"I'll deal with you in a little bit." Javier shook his head slightly.

A familiar fear shot through her when he turned his gaze on her. Unlike her own bright golden eyes, her father's were dark. Almost black, and completely devoid of compassion or kindness.

"As for you, dear daughter. I think your fiancé will be very happy to see you."

"No!" Konner lunged forward and slipped from the grip of his captors.

Dakota jumped from her chair, but before she could reach her mate, the two thugs jumped on him.

Dakota shrieked as they began beating him, but they were relentless in their assault. She willed him to stop resisting. And finally, bloody and broken, Konner stopped fighting back. It only took one thug this time to drag him to his feet and lock his arms behind his back.

Dakota bit back a sob when Konner wouldn't look at her. He hung his head and blood dripped from his injuries, to the floor beneath him.

Javier, who looked more entertained than put out, stepped toward her and grabbed her forearm with a pinch. "Don't even think about going anywhere. Dominic has been patient for far too long. We'll get this done right now."

Konner groaned but didn't attempt to struggle.

"Sam." Javier nodded in Konner's direction. "Did you get me that insurance?"

The man grinned, and Dakota shuddered.

"Right outside, boss."

"Excellent." He squeezed Dakota's arm until it hurt. "I'm not sure we'll need it." He sneered at her. "Since it appears the bear has a *thing* for the princess. But a little extra insurance never hurt, did it?"

Dakota worked hard to keep her face expressionless, but she feared it was already too late. She'd played her hand too early. Even if her father couldn't tell that Konner was her mate, he knew they were connected, and she didn't put it past him to hurt her to keep him in line.

She leaned into the bond, trying desperately to connect with Konner somehow. Finally, she felt it. A warm, peaceful sensation. He wasn't looking at her, but she could feel him. He was okay.

Through the bond, Dakota let the sensation of him and his love wash through her. He was unexpectedly calm, and if he was in control, she could be, too. It was hard to think that she'd ever doubted him for even a second.

It wasn't Konner's fault he was working for her father. He was doing it for his family.

Yes, he should have told her the truth. But she could see why he hadn't. He'd had his reasons for keeping the truth from her. And those reasons were becoming clearer by the second. He was trying to protect her. He would never hurt her.

Konner was her mate. He wouldn't let anything happen to her. Just as she wouldn't let anything happen to him. They would get out of there. They would leave her father behind once and for all. She hoped like hell she was able to convey her certainty through the bond in return.

Dakota's breathing began to even out as she focused on Konner and their connection. A moment later, whatever sense of peace she'd found was shattered as a fierce roar split the air.

Cressa.

Before Konner could stop it, his bear reacted when they brought his little sister into the room. A roar ripped from his throat and a second later, he was flat on his back, his head throbbing where he'd been pistol-whipped.

"Insurance."

King stood over him as he came to. He couldn't have been out long. Enough to make a point. His shifter healing had been kicked into overdrive, but Sam and his thugs were delivering enough regular blows to keep him subdued.

He forced himself to swallow the growl that threatened to tear from his throat. Just as he'd been forcing himself not to fight back. He didn't want to give King any reason to tie him up or just kill him to shut him up.

Konner didn't think he'd do that, though. King was too sadistic for that. And too fucking smart. It hadn't taken the Mafia father long to figure out why he'd lied about Dakota. They were connected. He might not know they were fated mates, but he knew they had feelings for each other. Konner had seen it in his eyes when he'd first made the connection.

No. He wouldn't end Konner's life. Not if he thought he could take any bit of pleasure from Konner's pain. And the best way to do that was to make him witness Dakota's pain.

And now Cressa's.

Fuck.

Slowly, Konner turned his head, a lightning flash of hot pain searing through his temple as he did so. King stood in front of Cressa. Her hands were bound, and she looked as if the assholes had beaten her. No doubt his sister would have fought. Brave. But dumb. Then again, she didn't have any idea what King and his men were capable of.

And he was going to make damn sure she didn't find out.

With one hand, King squeezed Cressa's cheeks. "You're a pretty little thing, aren't you?"

"Fuck you," Cressa spat at him, and just as quickly, King backhanded her across the face.

"Father!" Dakota lunged forward.

Konner tried to focus on the bond and get her to stay calm, but he wasn't strong enough. Either that, or she was ignoring him. He wouldn't blame her after everything that had happened, but he didn't believe that. He could feel her through their bond. Maybe they still had a lot to talk about, but Konner could feel her. They were on the same side. Always.

King raised his hand to strike his daughter but stopped short. "You should worry about yourself, princess. If I'm not mistaken, your fiancé is not pleased with your behavior. I'm sure you'll be begging for forgiveness soon enough."

Bastard.

Konner had never seen King interact with his daughter before, but it was every bit as disgusting as he'd imagined it to be.

Dakota visibly wilted in front of him and retook her seat.

"Now." King clapped his hands together. "We're just waiting for the guest of honor and—here he is."

The door opened once more and the man who could only be Dominic strode into the room. His presence commanded respect. From everyone but Konner.

Dominic was dressed all in black in clothing that no doubt cost more than Konner's apartment. His jet-black hair was slicked back from his face, revealing dark eyes that focused directly on Dakota.

Everything about the way he carried himself, the way he walked, the way he dressed...the man screamed *sadistic douche bag.* Konner would take extra pleasure in taking him down.

Cressa had wisely learned to keep her mouth shut. Konner had enough to worry about without worrying about her getting herself into a tighter mess. If they had any hope of escape, he was going to need everyone conscious.

Where the fuck was Knox?

Konner hated to admit it, but even he was having trouble figuring out just how he was going to take out three of King's men, plus the Mafia father himself, and now, the fucking fiancé. He was going to need help.

He took a moment to center himself and focus on the bond. He hoped like hell Dakota hadn't tuned him out completely. His instincts told him she hadn't. She was confused, that was easy enough to see, but it didn't take any kind of connection or bond to see that she was figuring things out quickly.

He willed her to stay calm. From across the room, he watched her take a deep breath and exhale slowly. She was working hard to be brave. Konner could see the way her fingers wrapped around her arm. She was doing a good job showing King and Dominic she wasn't afraid, but Konner could see the cracks. She was terrified. He'd fucking kill them for scaring his mate. And so help them if they laid a hand on her.

He took a deep breath and forced himself not to get off track. He couldn't afford any mistakes.

Dakota was focused on the alpha panther who was slowly stalking his way across the room toward her.

Stay calm. You're a fierce mountain lion shifter. Never forget that.

Her eyes flicked toward him, locking on his. The bond worked. She blinked slowly in acknowledgment and inhaled deeply before turning her attention back to Dominic. Her chin was set, tipped up in defiance, her eyes narrowed in challenge.

Fuck yes, kitten.

Konner smirked a little and quickly looked down before anyone noticed.

"I like my women with a little fire in them." Dominic's voice was low and smooth, every word spoken like a man who'd always gotten what he wanted. He reached out and took her chin in his hand. "It makes it more fun when I snuff out that flame for good."

Konner gritted his teeth and swallowed a growl.

"Fuck you." Dakota jerked to the side, freeing herself from his grip. When Dominic raised his hand to strike her, her own hand shot up and wrapped around his wrist. "Don't touch me."

With only a flick of his arm, Dakota went flying out of her chair and crashed to the floor.

Konner's muscles tensed in response, but he held himself back and leaned into the bond, hoping like hell she could feel him.

Breathe, kitten. Don't provoke him.

She coiled as if she were going to lunge up and attack the man, but thankfully, she sank back onto the floor and glared at Dominic while he laughed.

"Oh yeah," the asshole said. "You're going to be a lot of fun."

"Worth the wait then?"

Dominic spun to face King and snarled, "It's not done yet. And I'm quickly running out of patience."

"Then let's get on with it." King clapped his hands. "Hell, you can even have this one as a wedding gift."

He kicked at Cressa's leg, and Konner momentarily forgot himself when she cried out. A growl ripped from his throat. In retaliation, King punched his sister in the face hard enough to knock her unconscious.

He roared, but the thug holding him tightened his grip.

"Like I said, Stark. Insurance." King stalked toward him. "One more outburst, and I'll kill her."

Konner believed him.

Chapter Eighteen

FROM HER POSITION on the floor, Dakota curled her legs up to her chest and watched as the thug who'd been holding Konner's sister, who was now unconscious, dumped her in a heap on the floor. She'd never seen her father hit someone before. Not like that. It made her stomach turn, but it shouldn't have surprised her.

"Leave her," Javier ordered the man. "Get the judge. Let's get this done."

The marriage.

How could she ever have been naive enough to think she could just waltz back into her father's home and tell him good-bye? She should have just stayed hidden, where he couldn't get her.

But no. That wasn't a solution either. Not really.

Wasn't that really why she was there? She needed to remember that.

She never would have been free any other way. Not truly, if Konner found her. Knox found her.

Her father would never have given up. She'd always known that, only now she could see it clearly.

She would never be free of him. Not as long as he was alive. Or…

No way.

It was a crazy idea.

She scanned the room.

Was she brave enough to try?

For the moment, no one was paying any attention to her.

It might not even work. But there was only one way to find out.

She just needed a few more minutes.

Earlier, she'd felt Konner through their connection. It was a huge risk. But it was all they had. It was worth a try.

Stall them. Distract them.

She saw his eyes flutter, and his head dipped in a slight nod.

Konner struggled against his restrainer. "What are you going to do, King?" he taunted, pulling their attention back. "You think I give a shit about your daughter?"

Dakota's cougar snarled at his choice of words, but she ignored it. She waited and watched for a moment to be sure no one was paying attention to her while Konner continued to pull them in.

"You can have her," he said to Dominic. "If you're okay with sloppy seconds," he spat. "You didn't really expect your princess to be pure, did you?"

Dammit, Konner.

Dakota swallowed hard and, slowly, reached her hand into her coat pocket and clutched her phone. By touch, she entered the password to unlock it.

Across the room, Konner was drawing Dominic closer, too. "Because she's anything but pure." He leered, and Dakota swallowed hard, trying not to listen. "In fact," he continued, "maybe I could show you a thing or—"

The sound of crunching bone split the air, and Dakota had to force herself not to look. She took the opportunity of distraction to slip her phone out of her pocket and tap the button that would open Fuchsia's social media account. One more glance across the room confirmed that all eyes were on Konner, who, like a bobblehead doll, kept bouncing back for more abuse.

Quickly, Dakota pushed the button to start live streaming. While Konner took yet another hit, this one from her father, she propped the phone up on the built-in bookshelf, as high as she could reach, between two vases, and hoped like hell the angle was right to capture the events.

"You just don't know when to shut up, do you, Stark?"

Konner was still standing, but Dakota could tell it wouldn't be for long.

She watched as her father wound up to deliver another blow. Without waiting for the impact, as loud as she could, she said, "My real name is Angelica King."

Her father, fist in the air, turned to face her as she stood up. "That's your *only* name."

"Some people know me as Dakota," she continued, as if he hadn't spoken. "Many know me only as Fuchsia."

"Fuchsia?" Dominic scoffed, his attention also now turned toward her. "That sounds like a stripper's name."

"It's a color." She dismissed him with a shake of her head.

"This is ridiculous." Javier stepped up. "Your name is Angelica."

"And my father is Javier King." She spoke as clearly as she could and stepped toward the men. "Head of the King Mafia family in Vancouver." Hopefully their focus would remain on her and off her phone. She didn't think they'd be able to see it, but with any luck, if they did, hopefully there would already be enough people watching to make a difference.

"That's right." Her father was quickly losing his patience. "I'm your father. And as your father, I'm—"

"Forcing me to marry Dominic Dufort."

Javier's lips curled up into a wicked grin. "Is that what you're worried about?"

"There's nothing to worry about, princess." Dominic, whom she hadn't noticed come up next to her, grabbed her arm and yanked her toward his side.

Automatically, she recoiled.

"We're going to be a very happy couple."

Dakota pulled away from him. "You can't make me marry you."

He grabbed her and pulled her tight against his front. Her stomach flipped as he lowered his mouth to hers. "I can," he spat. "And I will." He pressed his mouth to hers in an aggressive and painful kiss. His tongue invaded her mouth and almost gagged her before he pulled back. "And if you don't like it." He shrugged. "It doesn't matter, because I will."

"This is a very important deal, Angelica. You will do as you're told."

"Important to who?" She once more yanked away from Dominic. This time, he let her go. "The family? The *Mafia family?*"

Her brain was working overtime to think of all the important details she could express to her live audience. She needed to give them as much information as possible without making Javier and Dominic suspicious. She'd never done anything like this before, but if she knew her audience as well as she hoped she did, they'd be completely invested in what was happening. Generally, when she did a spontaneous live video, her audience would share it wildly all over social media. It was almost as if they each wanted to be the first to let others know about Fuchsia's latest video. They were an audience hungry for content, and the best part was, they were devoted.

Dakota hoped like crazy that devotion would carry over today to get the live stream in front of the right eyeballs as quickly as possible.

She spun away from them and dropped her head in her hands, needing a moment to think.

"Angelica," her father's voice was infuriatingly patronizing and impatient, "don't be difficult. This is—"

"Look at me!" She lifted her head sharply and stared straight into the camera for a beat. "Look at me." She turned around. "Do I look like I'm being difficult?"

Dominic clicked his tongue. "You look like you need a few lessons in discipline."

Behind him, Dakota saw Konner stiffen momentarily before once more relaxing. She wished she had a better understanding of their mate bond and she could tell him what she was doing and be sure he understood, but she had every confidence that he'd already figured it out. Or if he hadn't, he would. They were running out of time.

"I *look* like a woman who doesn't want or need her father telling her what to do anymore." She screwed up all the confidence she could and stalked toward her *intended*. "I won't be any part of this." She took a breath and released it before continuing. "To think that both Javier King and Dominic Dufort are here, together in the King compound in North Vancouver. There's so much evil in one room."

"Angelica."

Her father's voice held a warning tone, but she ignored it. She only had one chance to make her point.

"It's bad enough that you steal from innocent people with your casinos," she continued. "I know I don't even know the half of it when it comes to the money laundering and the way you cash in on debts." Her eyes flickered to Konner and his sister, who started to stir on the ground. She didn't know the details of that, but Dakota could read between the lines. They were both paying for their father's mistake and her father's greed.

"I did what I had to do, Angelica." He took another step

toward her. "It's not my fault if the money was there for the taking. Someone was going to take it—it might as well have been me. And those who got in the way?" He laughed. He actually laughed. "Collateral damage."

She knew she was walking a very fine line as she continued. "The lives that have been lost because of the two of you and the way you think you can walk through the world doing whatever you want and taking whatever and whomever you want... I refuse to be—"

The slap hit her face hard enough to send her flying across the room. The last thing she remembered as she hit her head on the side of her father's massive oak desk was, *I hope it was enough.*

She was so brave. Maybe a bit reckless, but really fucking brave.

Konner had to force himself not to react to Dakota's words. He needed King's thugs to think he'd given up. It was working, too. The oaf, whose name he thought might be Dan, had relaxed his grip on his arms. King had sent Sam, and the other guy who had brought in Cressa earlier, to fetch the justice of the peace, or whoever was going to perform the sham of a wedding ceremony.

They weren't going to get a much better opportunity.

Dakota obviously recognized the opportunity as well. Across the room, she was starting to escalate things. King and Dominic were both starting to get fidgety, losing their patience with her. She was saying too much, but then again, maybe it was exactly what needed to be said to end this for good.

He had no idea how she was pulling it off, but he hoped like hell no one else noticed the little red light on her phone that indicated she was recording everything.

Konner caught a flash of movement out of the corner of his eye. It was brief, but he was sure it had been Knox at the window. It had to be. At least, he hoped like hell it was. Because a second later, Dominic raised his hand against Dakota, and Konner had had enough.

He let a roar rip from his throat, and, at the same time, he slammed his head backward into Dan's nose. The man let out a howl. No doubt he'd broken his nose. *Good.*

Konner didn't wait to find out. He lunged for Dominic and threw a punch that landed squarely in the man's jaw, sending him reeling backward. He didn't give him a moment to recover before he jumped on top of him and delivered another punch, and then another in a flurry of anger.

Behind him, he heard the window shatter as Knox finally joined the party. He vaguely registered the sounds of fighting between Knox and King, but he couldn't spare a moment to look.

Beneath him, Dominic was fighting with his claws out, delivering swipes that were slicing through his clothes and leaving searing cuts in his skin. "I should fucking kill you." Konner delivered a blow that slammed Dominic's head into the ground. He shifted to the side and kneeled his body weight onto the man's arm to stop the attack. Dominic howled in pain. More than anything, his bear wanted to take care of Dominic properly, but Dakota was recording. He couldn't risk it.

Behind him, a gunshot rang out, followed by a cry.

With Dominic properly pinned under him, Konner turned to see Knox lying on his side, clutching his leg. There was already a lot of blood beneath him. Knox would heal, but if the bullet hit an artery, he might not heal fast enough.

"That's enough, Stark."

Konner swallowed back a growl at the sight of King, his gun still drawn, but this time pointed at Cressa's head. She was starting to wake up, but not fast enough. Dan had recovered from the blow to his nose and was holding his sister up. Her head lolled back.

"I warned you, Stark. I'll kill her."

Konner heard the click of the gun as the hammer was cocked. Blood pounded in his ears, and he couldn't see straight. He had no doubt that the asshole would follow through on his threat without hesitation. He'd been around long enough to see him for the heartless, sadistic asshole he was.

In a flash, he worked out the distance in his head. He was too far away. He'd never be able to get to Cressa before King fired. And even if he could, they were outnumbered. But he had to try. Konner swallowed hard and was about to lunge toward them when a strong, but shaky voice behind him said, "Smile for the camera, *Dad.*"

Dakota.

Under him, Dominic groaned. Konner delivered another blow to his face, knocking him out again. No doubt the panther shifter would try to tear his throat out given half the chance. Fortunately for Konner, he had a massive size advantage over Dominic, never mind the fact that the Mafia king had spent most of his life having others do his dirty work, and clearly didn't have any actual fighting skills of his own. He'd been much easier to take down than Konner expected.

Still, he didn't underestimate him, as he turned to see Dakota. She stood with her phone in her hand now, the little red light still glowing. Blood poured from a wound over her left eye, but she didn't let it bother her as she walked toward them, moving the phone as she went. She looked fierce, and Konner felt a swell of love for his incredibly brave mate.

"Angelica, put your phone down. It's hardly the time for—"

"I'm live streaming everything, Father." She glanced down

at the screen. "And there are at least one hundred thousand viewers who are watching everything."

"What are you talking about?" King waved the gun, and Konner gritted his teeth. "You're not live streaming anything. And even if you were…what does it matter?"

"I am," she said calmly. "And I think you'd find it matters a great deal. Considering everything you've admitted." She quirked her lips up into a little smile. "Never mind the fact that you just attempted to murder my brother, live in front of hundreds of thousands of people."

King's eyes darted around. "Your brother?"

Dakota ignored him. "And now, you're threatening to kill an innocent woman. No doubt with a gun that isn't licensed or registered."

"You can't—"

"The police are on their way." Dakota stepped forward.

Konner watched as she scanned the room with her phone, making sure to capture the entire scene.

"And an ambulance," she added. "Hang in there, Knox." She turned the camera quickly on herself and quickly recited the address for the viewers and reiterated the need for help to arrive quickly before turning the camera around again. "It's over, Father. Drop the gun."

The sound of sirens in the distance quickly grew louder as they got closer. King must have heard them too, because, to Konner's surprise, he put the gun down and kicked it away.

"It's over," Dakota said again. And then almost to herself, added, "Finally."

Everything happened quickly after that. Moments later, the room and the entire King compound was descended on by a swarm of emergency personnel. King, Dominic, and his men were all put under arrest. It turned out that one of Fuchsia's most devoted followers was the daughter of a detective who had been looking into King and his operations for years. She'd paid enough attention around the dinner table to put two and two together, and had informed her mom as soon as she noticed Fuchsia's live feed.

The detectives had seen everything, and it looked as though justice was finally going to be served.

Knox and Cressa were attended to by the medics, but released when they were seen to have made a miraculous recovery. There weren't many humans who knew about shifters and their healing powers, but there were enough in the know that there were no uncomfortable questions asked.

Konner and Dakota were taken in for questioning, but Konner refused to let Dakota out of his sight. Never again. She'd been incredibly brave and had risked everything. It seemed to have worked out, this time. But Konner wasn't naive enough to realize that the situation could have turned out very differently. He could have lost his mate for good. And if that had happened...well, he refused to think about what the worst-case scenario would have looked like.

When they finally walked out of the police station together, Konner reached for her hand. She let him take it, but he didn't want to press his luck. He knew they had a lot of talking to do. He'd lied to her and, despite the fact that his reasons were perfectly valid at the time, he'd been wrong not to tell her from the beginning.

"Dakota?"

She turned to look at him. The cut over her eye had already begun to heal, but there was dried blood along her hairline and the bruising had faded into a yellow and purplish hue. She looked exhausted, but her golden eyes still held their sparkle.

Konner turned and took her other hand in his. "Dakota,"

he said again. "There's so much…I thought that maybe…" He dropped his head, overcome with emotion, and took a moment to collect his thoughts. When he looked up, there were tears shining in her eyes. "I'm so sorry, kitten. So incredibly sorry for not telling you—"

"Shh."

He shook his head. There was still so much to say. "I need you to know that—"

"I know, Konner." She squeezed his hands in hers and pulled him closer.

"You know?"

She nodded. "I can feel it." Dakota lifted his hand and pressed it to her chest. "I can feel exactly how you feel." She pressed her other hand over his chest. "Because I can feel it, too."

"I never should have lied to you—"

"Ssh," she said again, this time with a small smile. "No. You shouldn't have lied to me. But I understand now why you did. And I hope you understand why that was dumb."

He laughed. "Do I ever." Konner stepped toward her, needing to feel her in his arms. "I can't even tell you how scared I was that I'd lose you, Dakota. When I realized you'd gone back to—" He broke off and shook his head. "I've never felt such fear like that before, kitten." He cupped her cheek in his palm and stroked her skin. "I could never live with myself if something happened to you. I need you like I need air to breathe and—"

Again, he broke off and dropped his head, choked with emotion.

"Hey." She lifted his chin and forced him to look her in the eye. "Nothing's going to happen to me. I don't know if you noticed, but I can take care of myself."

Konner couldn't help it; he laughed and shook his head. "Don't I know it? Damn, woman, that was incredibly brave.

Maybe a bit foolish," he added. "But so fucking brave. You are amazing."

Dakota dropped her head so her forehead rested on his chest. "It's over now."

Konner wrapped her up in his arms and held her tight. It *was* over. All of it. Dakota was done running. From the sounds of it, and the sheer number of charges that were pending against him, her father wouldn't be getting out of jail any time soon. And when he did, all his assets had been seized. He couldn't harm her now. As for Dominic, even if he did want anything to do with the King family going forward, he was being held for extradition to the United States and was facing a laundry list of charges himself.

Dakota was truly free of them.

Which meant that Konner was too. With King gone, so was his family's debt, along with the hold he had over them. It really was over.

"I don't know about you." He kissed the top of her head. "But I can't think of anything I'd like better than to take you home."

Chapter Nineteen

HOME.

Predator Peak was home, and the moment Dakota and Konner finally pulled up in front of her small house on the edge of town, a sense of peace washed over her.

It had taken a few days before they were finally able to leave Vancouver. The detectives had asked them to stay close in case they had any more questions, and then there was the matter of clearing out the few possessions she wanted to take with her from the compound she'd grown up in.

Dakota would never again think of that prison as her *home*. When she finally walked out the front door, a small bag of her possessions in her hand, she didn't even look back. As far as she was concerned, that part of her life was behind her. Hopefully for good.

Konner hadn't left her side throughout everything. She knew he felt terrible about lying to her about his true identity and his connection to her father, but she wasn't upset with him, not after the way he'd risked everything to save her. How could she stay mad? Besides, she could see the hold her father had over him and his entire family, and the fact that

Konner had been willing to do what he did and dedicate his life to paying off his father's debt made her love him even more.

There wasn't a doubt in her mind that he was committed to her. He was her mate, and she'd never felt the bond as strong as she did now. It was as if he were with her all the time. A warmth in her chest that grounded her to something bigger.

But he was also dedicated to his family. Dakota had no experience with a family who loved each other so fiercely that they would give up their entire lives to save the others. It was mind-boggling at first, but after she'd met Cressa properly and Konner's mom, Tess, she had a deeper understanding.

They'd both welcomed her into their lives so completely and without reservation, it had been hard to leave.

But the appeal of getting home and being alone with her mate—finally—was more than enough incentive to help her pack up the car and begin the long journey home.

"Here we are." Konner put the rental car in park but didn't turn the key off. "I'll help you inside and then you can get—"

"You're coming in." It wasn't a question.

"Oh, kitten. I'm coming in all right." His grin was slow and sexy. "I meant it when I said that I don't plan on letting you out of my sight for very long."

He reached across the console and squeezed her thigh. His touch sent a shot of heat through her, directly to her core. It really had been too long since they'd been alone. Sleeping on his mother's fold-out bed didn't really afford them the privacy they'd so badly needed.

"I'll help you in with your bags and then I—"

"You just said you were coming in."

"And I am. But there's something I need to take care of first."

She eyed him carefully and nodded in understanding. Konner told her that Nolan had lent him the money to pay off her father, no questions asked. She also knew he was eager to repay him.

"Okay." She leaned over and kissed him on the cheek. "But you don't need to see me inside. I think I've proved I'm fully capable of taking care of myself."

Konner growled and grabbed her and pulled her in close for a deep kiss that threatened to melt her into a puddle of desire right there. *Damn.* She was going to be counting the minutes until she had him alone.

"And you're so fucking sexy when you do," he said when he released her. She bit her bottom lip, and he groaned. "Go," he ordered. "Or I'll never let you leave."

She winked. "Promises, promises."

Dakota forced herself out of the car. The sooner he took care of what he needed to, the sooner they could have a proper homecoming. Knox had returned to Predator Peak the day before to get his things and move into the place Konner had been renting until he figured out what he wanted to do next.

She waited until Konner drove off before turning toward the house. There was extra satisfaction in returning to the life she'd built for herself now that she was completely free. The last time she'd been here, she'd been hiding. In more ways than one.

But now...

Dakota set her bag down and pulled her phone out of her pocket. She'd only made one other post on Fuchsia's social media accounts since her dramatic live stream, and that was only to thank everyone who'd contacted the authorities—which had turned out to be thousands of people—and to let her followers know that she was doing well and would be back online soon.

She couldn't think of a better time.

With a flick of a button, Dakota was live streaming, this time with the camera facing her and her entire face in the shot.

It felt both terrifying and amazing. "Hi everyone. It's Fuchsia here." She and Konner had discussed the need to continue to use the pseudonym and not to share any personal details with her audience, especially now that it had grown exponentially. The threat of her father may have been neutralized, but that didn't mean there weren't other weirdos out there. Better safe than sorry. "I just wanted to take a minute to pop on," she continued. "And let you all know that I'm home now and doing better than ever."

Her smile filled the screen, and her eyes sparkled back at her as she filmed. "I know in the past, I've focused only on very specific eye makeup looks, and if you've been following everything that's been happening with me lately, you'll see that there's been a good reason for that." She laughed. "But things are going to change. I just need a few days to settle back in at home, and then I promise you, I'll be back with some all-new full-face looks."

Her eyes flickered to where the comments had begun coming in and she smiled. "And I'll answer every single one of your comments." She hoped that was a promise she could keep. There were already so many. "Stay tuned, lovelies." Dakota blew a kiss to the camera and ended the stream.

Konner found Nolan across town, working on a renovation project. He let himself into the house and followed the sound of hammering to the upstairs bedroom. "Hey." He waited until Nolan put the hammer down. "Sorry to interrupt."

"Konner!" Nolan wiped his hands on his jeans and moved across the room to pull Konner into a back-slapping hug. "Damn. It's good to see you, man. I couldn't believe it when I heard about Dakota's—or should I say Angelica's—"

"No. It's Dakota."

Nolan nodded. "I couldn't believe it when I heard about her family and everything that went down. Fuck. I'm glad you're all okay. Ivy was a mess when she heard. It was everything I could do to keep her from getting in the car and heading to the coast."

Konner laughed at the idea of a very pregnant, very hormonal wolf shifter driving to the coast to take care of King and his men. He shrugged. Maybe it wouldn't have been such a bad idea.

"It was all pretty crazy, and Dakota..." He shook his head. "She's fierce, man. I mean, I couldn't even believe it. She was incredible."

"Pretty kick-ass," Nolan agreed. "Well, it's good to have you back. I assume you *are* back..."

"We're back. And very happy about it. In fact, I just dropped Dakota off at home, but I wanted to take care of this before anything else." He reached into his pocket and handed Nolan the stack of bills he'd borrowed less than a week earlier. "Thank you for this."

"You didn't need it?"

Konner shook his head. "Turns out debts are forgiven when the collector is a Mafia crook who's headed to prison for what hopefully is a very long time."

Nolan laughed. "Damn, if you'd told me what it was for—"

"You didn't ask, remember?"

He nodded and took the money. "I remember. And I'd lend it to you again, no questions asked."

"I appreciate that, man. More than you'll ever know."

Nolan waved him away. "Forget it. We're pack. I told you that."

Konner laughed. "And I told you, I'm a bear. We don't have—"

Nolan held up his hammer to stop him from finishing the

sentence. "You *do* have pack, Konner. Because you're here. You're in Predator Peak with us. You have Dakota, obviously. And Knox, whether you want him or not."

Konner shook his head with a chuckle. Ever since he sacrificed himself to save Cressa, the mountain lion was growing on him.

"And me, and Ivy and the baby whenever she comes." Nolan was still talking. "And Jager and Ruby, too."

Konner nodded. "And Cressa and my mom."

"See?" Nolan dropped the hammer to his side again. "Pack. Maybe you call it something different, but around here, it's pack. And we'd do anything to protect our pack." He grinned. "Including lending you large sums of money, no questions asked."

Konner shook his head in gratitude.

"Although, next time," Nolan said, "if you're going into battle with a friggin' Mafia boss, maybe you could let us know so we could give you some backup." He shook his head and Konner couldn't help but laugh.

"Backup *would* have been a good idea." He sighed and grew serious again. "But there won't be a next time. It's over."

"I'm glad to hear it, man. Now you and your mate can get to the serious business of solidifying that bond of yours."

"That's exactly what I intend to do." Konner nodded in perfect agreement. "Hey. It might be a bit too soon, but I need to ask you for one more favor."

"You're not sleeping, are you?"

Dakota opened one eye to see Konner, propped up on one elbow, looking down at her. He walked his fingers up her hip and over her stomach. His travels paused at her breast long enough to circle her nipple and give it a quick pinch, which sent a shot of desire straight between her legs.

"Mmmm. I'm definitely not sleeping."

He grinned wickedly and moved so he was completely overtop of her. They'd spent the entire morning on a blanket next to the stream behind the hunting cabin that Nolan had lent them. It had become their favorite spot in the week they'd spent up on the mountain alone. Although, every part of the tiny cabin and spectacular surroundings were their favorites, and that was mostly because they were finally alone together.

"You know what I think?" Konner bent to kiss her gently before moving his mouth to her neck.

"I could guess." She giggled and wiggled her hips up against his hard cock.

"Okay," he conceded. "Do you know what I think besides the fact that I want to be inside you?"

Her body vibrated in need at his words. They had spent the last few days making love as if it were their job. They'd learned every inch of each other's body and connected with each other on a level that Dakota hadn't even known was possible.

"I couldn't even begin to guess." She pressed her breasts up, and he moaned, pulling his attention away from her neck to focus on her nipples.

"I think we were wrong." He sucked a nipple between his lips, and it was Dakota's turn to moan. Wet heat rushed between her legs as he once more, easily, made her ready.

"Wrong about what?"

Konner lifted his head so he could look into her eyes. "About solidifying the mate bond. It's not just for wolves at all. We needed this."

Dakota couldn't disagree that the time alone to just *be* with each other hadn't been amazing. It had been the best way to unwind and refocus after all the chaos of the beginning of their relationship. But...she shook her head.

"You disagree?"

"It's been amazing." She sighed as he lowered himself so the tip of his cock pressed between her legs. "You've been amazing."

"So you don't disagree?"

"No," she said. "I do. Because as nice as it's been, we didn't *need* it. Not the way Nolan and Ivy did. That's not how cougar shifters work. And you already told me that bear shifters are *at first sight* kinda of people."

He chuckled and kissed her again. "It's true. I just needed to lay eyes on you to know you were mine forever. Just like that, I was done for." He pulled up. "But it wasn't like that for you."

It wasn't a question, but she shook her head anyway. "Well, yes and no." Dakota traced her fingers down his back to rest on his firm ass. "You already know the way I reacted to you."

"Mmm. You mean the way you *still* react to me."

She smacked him playfully. "Right."

"But seriously though, something changed for you," Konner said. "If it wasn't this last week together, what was it?"

Dakota blew out a breath with a smile and reached up to cup her mate's face. "For us, and maybe for me especially, it's all about trust. I know that now more than ever. Cougar shifters are known for being independent and loners."

"You don't say." He grinned. "I told you I'd seduce you."

She shook her head and rolled her eyes a little. "But seriously, it's harder for us to let others in. Even when I knew you and I were fated, my cat was still standoffish."

"Standoffish?" He raised an eyebrow. "Because that's not how I'd describe those first few—"

"It's hard to explain." She knew he was teasing. Cat shifters were different. More complicated. Even when she'd *known* he was hers and she was his, there was still a sliver of doubt buried underneath everything. A doubt that vanished when he'd risked everything for her. Now, mind, body, and soul, there was no doubt in her mind.

"I'm teasing." He stroked her cheek. "And only because I know how simple bears can be." He flashed her a smile. "And you, kitten, are anything but simple."

"It's true." She winked. "But I actually think this is kind of simple. Because, with you, it's different. My whole life, I've never felt safe. I've always been on guard. Alone, against…well, everyone. But with you, there's no longer any doubt." She closed her eyes and took a breath. "With you, I'm…" She let the thought drift away, suddenly self-conscious.

"What? With me, you're what, kitten?"

She looked up at him through a veil of unshed tears. "With you, I'm home."

He kissed her deeply until the tears slipped down her cheeks. She lifted her hips, craving all of him. Konner happily complied, sinking himself deep inside her.

They made love slowly. Dakota's climax was a slow build until finally, her full body tightened; she squeezed her eyes shut and let the explosive sensations take over completely. Konner's own release was just as intense a moment later before he slipped off her and rolled to his back, pulling her up onto his chest.

"I'll always be your home, kitten." He stroked her hair away from her face and down her back. "Always."

"I know." She snuggled deeper into the crook of his arm and a low rumble started low in her gut. It took her a minute to realize that for the first time in her life, she was truly happy and content. She was purring.

Epilogue

THREE WEEKS LATER...

"I can't remember the last time I saw so much pink in one place."

Dakota turned, a tissue paper flower in her hand, to see her mate, eyes wide open, staring open-mouthed at the corner of the bar she'd been entrusted to decorate.

"I might have gone a little bit overboard." She shrugged and handed Konner the flower. "Can you hang this up?"

"Where?" Konner spun slowly and shook his head. "Unless you want me to put it on the bar, but—"

"No." Jager shot him a look from where he stood behind the bar, drying glasses. "I have to draw the line at the actual bar," he said. "It's sacred."

"I don't know about sacred." Dakota popped a hip and batted her eyelashes that were extra-long for the occasion in his direction. She didn't really expect him to budge, but it was fun to push him to the brink. "The bar could use a little—"

"Dakota. No. I still have actual customers today." He

dropped his shoulders and shook his head a moment later, defeated. "Fine."

Dakota squealed, and Konner laughed. "Should I be worried that you're wielding your feminine charms on him?"

"Oh, baby." With a pink balloon in each hand, she wrapped her arms around her mate's neck and kissed him thoroughly. "Never. You know I only have eyes for you."

He held her close and kissed her again before letting her go.

"Besides," she said over her shoulder as she made her way to the bar. "My feminine charms have nothing to do with it. Jager is only letting me do this because it's for Ivy."

The bartender nodded. "It's true. She's ridiculously huge with that kid. Everything is just about keeping Ivy happy right now until my little niece makes her appearance."

"Don't let her hear you say that," Dakota warned him as she taped the balloons to the bar and quickly added two tissue paper flowers before he could say no. "Even if it's true, I would not be brave enough to say anything remotely about her size."

"Whose size?" Ruby, Jager's daughter, ran out from under the bar and greeted Dakota with a hug. "Auntie Ivy? She's *huge*." Ruby held her arms out and opened her eyes wide until they all laughed.

"Do not let her hear you say that," Jager admonished his daughter, but Dakota didn't miss the smile.

"I promise I'm almost done decorating, Jager. I'll get all this cleaned up. The guests of honor should be here any moment."

She left him at the bar with Ruby and returned to her supplies and Konner, who was trying and failing to put together one of the tissue paper flowers.

"How do these things—"

"I don't need that one." She took it from his hand. "I maybe did go a little bit overboard, didn't I?"

Konner wrapped an arm around her waist and pulled her close. "You definitely did. She'll love it."

"I hope so." Dakota bit her bottom lip. "I just really wanted Ivy to feel special today. With everything that's been going on with me, and...well, with everything, too much of the focus was taken off her. And really, she's going to be a mom. She deserves to have all the focus on her."

"Kitten?" Konner spun her so she faced him. He lifted her chin with a finger, so she looked up at him.

It didn't matter how many times she was in that position; it still sent a little thrill through her when she looked up at her big, strong bear.

"Ivy knows how much you love her and this baby."

"I know, but—"

"It's okay. She's your best friend, and she understands that things have been crazy for you."

Crazy was a ridiculous understatement for what had happened since her live stream when she outed herself. Fuchsia's brand had absolutely exploded. When they finally came down the mountain from their little *retreat*, Dakota's inbox had been overflowing with all kinds of offers. Everything from makeup endorsement deals to modeling jobs. There were even a number of people who wanted to make a movie about her life or write a book based on the true events. Together, they'd worked through all the offers, rejecting a lot of them, but accepting enough of them to keep her busy for years. And the money she'd be making was more than enough for Konner to be able to focus on his writing. As soon as he was done with his first novel, they were going to work together on putting Dakota's story into words.

"Crazy or not," Dakota said, "today is about Ivy."

"And Nolan."

"Right, right. And Nolan, too." She winked and gave him

another kiss before turning to see Konner's mother, Tess, walk through the door. "Oh good, your mom's here."

Dakota and his mother got along so well, it was as if they'd known each other for years. In fact, Konner was pretty sure his mother liked his mate more than she liked him. Not that he cared. The only thing he cared about were the smiles on each of their faces. And they'd both been doing a lot of that in the last few weeks. Watching Dakota blossom after breaking free from her father's hold once and for all had been miraculous. She glowed from within, and Konner knew it was only just the beginning now that she didn't have to hide anymore.

It hadn't taken much convincing to get Tess to move up to Predator Peak with them. There was nothing left for her in Vancouver. She'd only stayed as long as she had because King had more or less held them hostage. All she wanted to do with her retirement was relax, sew for fun, and…as she loved to remind him…play with grandchildren.

It hadn't been quite as easy to get Cressa to commit to moving to Predator Peak. Now that King and his hold over the family were gone, she'd set her sights on traveling before her last semester at school started. Konner couldn't blame her, but it didn't change the fact that he'd prefer to have her close, where he could keep an eye on her. Still, he had to remind himself that she was safe now. Cressa didn't need him looking after her.

Konner scanned the gathering of mostly people he didn't know yet, or had met only once or twice before. He glanced across the table to see his mother coloring with Ruby before getting up. Konner would love nothing more than to give his mother plenty of grandchildren to dote on. But they weren't in a hurry. Not that he wasn't enjoying practicing. He snuck up behind Dakota, who was arranging the presents on a side table, and snuck a quick kiss. "The party is a success," he whispered in her ear. "You're amazing and a great friend." He gave her another quick kiss and quickly retreated to the bar where the men had gathered.

"What are you doing over here?" he asked Nolan as he gratefully accepted a beer from Jager. "I thought this was a couples thing."

His friend shook his head and took a sip of his beer. "This is an Ivy thing." Nolan's eyes shone with love as he watched his mate. "She needed this. The last few weeks have been...*a lot*." He shook his head and sipped his beer. "This pup can't come soon enough."

"You're going to be a great father, man." Knox slapped Nolan on the back as he joined them. "Sorry I'm a little late." He held up a hand to Jager when he offered him a beer. "I'm technically on duty. Covering a shift at the local department."

"You've been working a lot." Konner greeted the man with a half hug and a slap on the back. Their friendship had come a long way after the showdown with King, and it didn't hurt that he wasn't living in their house anymore.

Knox shook his head. "Fire season, man. I'm just happy to help out where I can."

"We're lucky to have you," Nolan said, and Jager agreed.

"Very lucky. The forest fires seem to get a little worse every year."

After coming back from Vancouver, Knox didn't know what he wanted to do, or where he wanted to go, but he and Dakota both agreed he should stay close, at least for a little while, so they could make up for lost time and get to know each other properly. When it was revealed that Knox had fire-fighting experience, he was snapped up by the local volunteer department as well as the forest firefighting team. Surrounded by forest the way they were in Predator Peak, there was no shortage of work.

Konner lifted his glass of beer and turned to survey the bar. "It's pretty busy in here," he said. "Aside from the baby shower, of course." There were still a lot of people he didn't know in town, but he was slowly getting to recognize more faces.

Across the room was a group he'd never seen before, most of them with striking red hair. "Hey. They're new," he said over his shoulder. "Visitors?"

Jager made a noise that might have been a chuckle. "I don't know if you've noticed, Konner, but we don't really get a lot of visitors around here. That's the Warner family. They own a large property on the south end of town, on Quartz Lake. But they don't generally spend much time up here. Warner moved the family to the city years ago when the girls were little."

Konner turned to see Jager scratch his chin in thought.

"Hell, they've got to be about twenty-three, twenty-four, now. It was all before my time. I only know the little I know from Bruce Warner himself. Turns out they had other land in the family, closer to the city. Developed that into a golf course of all things and now they're..." He rubbed his fingers together and raised his eyebrows. "Good for them, though. They still come up here a couple times a year. Pretty nice—"

"You'll do."

Konner turned to see a young, redheaded woman crash into Knox. She wrapped her slender arm around his waist. They both turned to look at each other at the same time. Konner saw the reaction in Knox as it happened. His body stiffened, his eyes grew wide, and his nostrils flared as he inhaled sharply.

The female, who was clearly intoxicated, simply smiled. "Oh yes," she said, her voice slipping over the words. "You'll do nicely."

Knox was visibly uncomfortable. Yet somehow he managed to swallow and ask, "Do for what?"

"For my boyfriend." She stood on her tiptoes to press a quick kiss on his cheek. Despite being almost half his size, she easily pulled him off his stool. "Come on. It'll be easy. I promise."

Thank you for reading Seducing His Fate! I hope you enjoyed Dakota and Konner's story.

Who is the redhead in the bar? And why does she need Knox to be her *boyfriend?* Knox's story is next. Find out what happens next in Claiming His Fate

For more sexy shifters, make sure you check out The Bears of Grizzly Ridge
Save 50% on the entire series today!

Read an excerpt of His to Protect next

His to Protect

Please enjoy this excerpt of His to Protect from E.R. Aitken/Elena Aitken's original shifter series, Bears of Grizzly Ridge

CHAPTER One

Axel Jackson surveyed the land on the ridge and all he and his brothers had accomplished in the last nine months: The individual cabins tucked among the trees where he and his brothers lived. The barn that held a few trail riding horses. And of course the main lodge—the Den, they called it—that housed the guest rooms and main gathering spaces. They'd worked hard building a place they could call home. They'd had to.

More than that, they'd created a place they could build a life. If you called banishment from everything they'd known a life. But he did. As the eldest brother, and the alpha, there was no other choice.

He held the letter from his grandfather in his hand. The

same letter he'd carried with him for almost a year. The patriarch of the clan, Gordon Jackson, was still old school when it came to communication. But it didn't matter how he chose to communicate; the message was just as old school.

Axel read the words he already knew by heart.

"Your failure to protect your clanmate, your sister, has resulted in your banishment from Jackson Valley. Until which time you and your brothers are able to return Kira, unharmed, to her proper clan, you will no longer be welcome in the Valley or in the Clan."

He should rip it up and throw it into the wind. Instead, he folded it carefully along the timeworn crease lines. And just in time.

"I told you to throw that damn thing away," his brother Luke growled as he joined him on the ridge. His nakedness meant he'd recently been in his bear form. His preferred form. As shifters, they lived by a different code. Another reason the brothers had chosen the ridge to settle away from the others.

"Better yet," the youngest of the Jackson brothers, Kade, came to stand by Axel, "burn it."

Axel tucked it away into his pocket; Luke scoffed and shook his head. His scruffy, too-long long hair covered his eyes, but Axel could still see the disapproval there. "I don't know why you bother," he said. "The old man doesn't give a shit about us. He cast us out, the same way he cast out our parents. Giving him even a moment of our time is too much."

Everything his brother said was true. It wasn't the first time their grandfather had cast out a member. When their mother, Tonia, had fallen in love and subsequently chosen their father, Mark Chapman, who hailed from a rival clan, Gordon hadn't hesitated to banish her as well. Axel remembered very little about their parents, but he remembered more than the rest of them; he was five when they'd been sent back to the Jackson clan to live with their grandfather, and made to take the Jackson name again, forsaking the Chapman clan. He didn't know why or how it had come to pass, because no one would talk about it, but the fact remained: their grandfather was the only family they had.

"He's still family," he said to his brothers. "*Our* family."

"No," Kade said. "Family doesn't disown family because of a choice their sister makes." He winced and looked out over the ridge. Talking about Kira was hardest for Kade. As her twin brother, he felt the most that he'd let her down. Or perhaps that she'd been the one to let him down by choosing a mate in the first place. She'd known the consequences of her actions: alpha females in the Jackson clan didn't choose their own mates. Period. It was important to protect the lineage of the clan, and it was about more than producing cubs; it was more a business transaction between clan leaders than anything else. Which meant the granddaughter of the alpha male was promised. Not that it had mattered to Kira. She'd fallen in love. No matter what the cost had been to anyone else.

"Bear families do." Axel knew he was wasting his breath. It was the same argument they'd had for months. Ever since they'd tracked Kira the way they were told to. Only, instead of bringing her back to the clan the way their grandfather had commanded, they'd left her to live with her mate and his Kodiak clan. After hearing her story of fated mates, and how it felt as if their souls had chosen each other, the brothers agreed they had to leave her alone. All three of them had differing opinions about mating, but one thing none of them could deny was that forcing her to go with them and leave her mate would have been devastating to Kira. Never mind the war it likely would have sparked between the clans. None of the brothers were willing to do it. They'd decided then and there that together they'd accept whatever punishment their grandfather doled out.

No one had expected banishment.

Axel ran his hands through his thick hair. It had been

months since he'd had it cut. A benefit to living on the ridge, as far as he was concerned. The bear in him preferred to live a bit wilder. Just not as wild as Luke, who still sat next to him naked, one leg bouncing restlessly. He was itching to take his leave so he could shift back into his bear and run through the woods. Luke was much harder to tame. The ridge lifestyle suited him most of all. He'd had the easiest time making the transition. Except when it came to potential mates. But that was part of the sacrifice. There were no females on the ridge. They were alone. Mating was less and less of an option.

A mate would calm the bear in all of them. And as the wildest of the three, Luke stood to benefit the most from mating. Not that he'd admit it. In fact, Luke would vehemently deny that he needed anything but the wilds of Montana and the freedom to do what he wanted. Kade sought his relief, however temporary, in the arms of whatever females he could find, driving down into town as often as he could. He'd be the hardest of all of them to convince that a mate could be a good thing. He'd seen firsthand the damage taking a mate could do, and as hardheaded as he was, there was no changing his mind.

As far as Axel was concerned, he wouldn't rule it out if the right female somehow appeared. Not that it was likely.

Whatever. He shook his head to focus on the task at hand. There was no point dwelling on what couldn't be changed. "Is everything ready?"

Kade turned back to face him. The quietest of the three, sullen and almost angry, he'd become even more withdrawn in the last nine months. His dark eyes always looked a little haunted, a little sad. It was the loss of Kira. Twin bears had a unique bond, one even Axel couldn't hope to understand. It would be better if he let himself grieve her loss. If he'd let himself feel anything. But Kade seemed to have inflicted his own brand of punishment upon himself. "I brought the last of the supplies up on my last run to town. Everything should be in place. All we need now are guests."

When they'd decided to stay on the ridge, the brothers had come up with the idea to create an eco-tourism lodge that focused on hiking in the summer and backcountry skiing in the winter. It would be the first of its kind in Montana: rugged enough to appeal to the adventurous spirit, but cushy enough to be an upscale destination. It was the perfect compromise for the brothers. They may not be able to go home to Jackson Valley to the lives they'd left behind, but it wouldn't stop them from creating new ones.

"It's taken care of." Axel smiled. "We have some registered guests coming later in the week, but you guys are going to love this…"

"What are we going to love?"

"Try to restrain your bear for a few days," he said to Luke. "Because I secured a travel journalist from LA who's going to write a feature on Grizzly Ridge for *Lifestyles Magazine*."

"No shit?" That impressed Luke the way Axel knew it would.

"It's true. And she's going to be here in the morning with a guest. So seriously, rein in your bear."

Luke grumbled and kicked the ground, but Axel knew he'd do as he was told. They may have chosen the ridge for its remoteness and ability to shift into their bear form whenever they needed to, but now that there would be humans around, everyone was going to have to be a lot more careful.

Harper Bentley pulled into her garage and closed it behind her before she got out of the car. The thought of staying inside with her vehicle running flashed through her brain for a second. But only a second. She wouldn't give that asshole husband of hers the satisfaction.

Ex-husband.

Well, maybe not yet. But soon. Very soon.

Harper slammed the door to the garage and entered the relative peace of her home. Relative being the key word. Nothing about her house was peaceful. It was cold and glass and…decidedly not hers. It was Trent's. He'd designed and built it for appearances. Just like everything else in his life.

Until now.

With a sigh of disgust, Harper grabbed a bottle of wine from the rack, quickly popped the cork and poured herself a big glass before once more pulling the newspaper from her purse. It was already open to page four. The society pages. *Where everyone who was anyone made an appearance.* That's what Trent always said and look at him now. By the size of the photo, it was clear that Trent Bentley, co-owner of Bentley Images and Public Relations, was definitely someone. A very *gay* someone.

She tipped the glass back and swallowed half the contents easily in one gulp.

Trent's coming out was already a social sensation. Everyone was talking about it. Too bad they were also talking about her and how as the operating partner of Bentley Images, Harper Bentley clearly didn't have any kind of handle on image or public relations. It hadn't taken long for the media to spin everything in favor of Trent, the sophisticated and trendy gay man, braving society and coming out with his boyfriend, Blake Johnson. Which meant that same media had also done a superior job portraying Bentley as the dumpy, unaware, and completely clueless public relations representative who obviously couldn't handle any of her high-profile clients if she couldn't even handle herself. It had taken less than an hour after Trent's *big reveal* to go public for her phone to ring with five of her biggest clients dropping her.

"No doubt to go to the dark side," she muttered and finished off the rest of her wine. And it hadn't taken long for the reporters to get a hold of that information, too. Professionally, she was effectively dead. Never mind personally, not that Trent's sexual orientation had been much of a surprise. However, his betrayal had been.

Harper grabbed the bottle to pour herself another glass. "Oh, screw it." Forgoing the glass, she tipped the bottle up to her mouth.

"Nicely done."

The voice startled her and she choked on the wine. When she recovered from the ensuing coughing fit, she turned and glared at her best friend, Nina. "That wasn't nice."

"I'm the least of your problems," she said. "Besides, you gave me a key for a reason. I wasn't about to let you drink yourself into oblivion by yourself."

Harper pushed the bottle away. Nina was right. She was infuriating, but she was right. There was a reason they'd been best friends for years. "How did you know?"

"About the drinking? Or Trent?"

"Both." She thought better of her hasty decision and reached for the bottle again, but Nina held it out of reach.

"You know I've known about Trent for years." Harper nodded and didn't look up. They'd both known. But not right away. At first, it just seemed as though he just hadn't wanted to have sex. He was too tired, or not feeling good, or had a bad back. But then it was other things, too. On the rare occasions they actually did have sex, it was terrible. More than terrible. Harper may not have had a lot of experience with men, but she knew enough to know it was supposed to be better than that. They'd only been married two years when Trent finally admitted he'd married her as a cover. She'd been hurt, certainly. She should have left him then and she knew it. But something kept her, and as loathe as she was to admit it, that something was low self-esteem. She'd always been so strong in every other way, but when it came to feeling attractive or desirable, well, that was different. If she left Trent in search of something *more*, there wasn't any guarantee she'd find it. At least if she stayed, she'd have *something*. It was weak and she knew it. Over the years, she hated herself a little bit more for not allowing herself to go after what she deserved. But it became a vicious cycle she just couldn't seem to get out of.

Not that it was all bad. Their business was finally taking off. They were successful, getting more clients all the time. They worked well together. They were partners, friends, and their relationship was good.

Except for that one small detail.

She should have known once he'd met Blake it would only be a matter of time. He'd had boyfriends over the ten years they'd been married. Most of them discreet, but Blake had been different. *Dammit.* She should have been strong enough to leave him years ago. On her own terms. She should have been — "Give me the wine."

Nina shook her head. "No deal. I know this sucks and you're probably sitting there thinking of all the things you should have done differently." Harper shrugged. "But getting drunk isn't going to help."

"It's not going to hurt." She glared at her best friend. "But you're right. It's not the solution." The actual solution came to her in a flash and she pushed up from the chair to head for the fridge. "It's not like I have an image to worry about anymore. I'm going to eat whatever I want. Starting with this." She pulled out half a cheesecake that Trent had brought home a few nights before. Likely to torture her. Knowing she couldn't eat it on her diet. Her perpetual diet. It didn't seem to matter what she did—she had curves. Too many curves for Los Angeles, that was for sure.

Screw it. Her career was already circling the drain. Harper grabbed a fork and dug in, savoring the first bite.

"Well, at least share with me." Nina took the fork from her hand and took her own bite before she handed it back. "Because I have just the medicine you need."

Harper raised her eyebrows. "I don't know if drugs are really the answer right now, Nina."

"Stop it." Nina smacked her and laughed. "I'm totally serious."

"And what is the medicine you offer exactly? Because I need something."

"I have an assignment to do, and the offer was for two people. You're going to be my plus one." Nina was a travel writer and always jetting off to fabulous places where she was wined and dined. And got paid for it. Harper could definitely go for some wining and dining. Especially if it was far away from Los Angeles. Nina grabbed the fork again, but instead of taking another bite, she tossed it in the sink. "Come on. You have to pack. We're leaving first thing in the morning."

"What?" Harper let herself be dragged into the bedroom. She had neither the strength nor the desire to stop it. Especially if it meant a lavish holiday. "Where are we going?"

Nina turned and grinned. "Montana, baby."

Something was in the air.

Axel hadn't been able to sleep and it wasn't just the anticipation of their first guests. It was something else. Something in his blood that had kept him up. His bear was restless. He had too much to do, and the helicopter was due to land in less than an hour with the journalist. He couldn't afford to run off into the woods to satiate the animal inside him. There wasn't time.

Still…he couldn't afford not to.

Naked, Axel stepped outside into the dewy summer morning. Even on what would be a hot day, the mornings in the mountains were still cool. *Perfect.* He left behind the steps of his cabin and shifted seamlessly into his bear as he took off for the woods in long, lumbering strides.

He wouldn't be gone long. Just long enough to calm his bear.

As soon as he hit the trees, he increased his pace, pushing himself farther, harder, faster. His muscles strained with the effort and the exertion was just what he needed to quiet his brain and soothe his spirit.

A scent on the air caught his attention. Luke was somewhere in the distance but he wasn't surprised. Luke spent as much time as possible in his bear form and with the impending arrival of guests on the ridge, the opportunity to shift wouldn't be as forthcoming. Not that Axel was worried about it. They'd all lived among humans in the valley. It had never been a problem. Well, not really.

Where Luke was concerned, there was always a problem or two. All he needed to do was minimize them, at least while guests were around.

Axel growled and snuffed the air as he continued to lumber through the woods. He slowed his pace and pulled up as he arrived at the edge of the forest where the sky opened up to the valley below. The view never failed to calm him. Whenever he was worked up about something, he somehow always found his way to the edge of the mountain to find perspective. He sat heavy on his haunches and inhaled the fresh morning air. In his bear, all his senses were heightened, a little more alive. It generally made it easier to relax, but the stillness he'd hoped for didn't come right away. He took another breath. An eagle shrieked as it soared through the valley.

Still, his bear couldn't be calmed. Not the way he needed it to be.

And he knew why.

At thirty and the oldest of the brothers, Axel was due to take a mate first. In fact, he should have found one years ago. It was the only way for shifters to keep their animal side satiated. But even before banishment, he hadn't found a female who was right for him. Of course, his grandfather, the alpha of the clan, had tried to impose upon him a deadline to find his own mate, or he'd be mated to a female from a neighboring clan. The bloodline had to be preserved. Not that it mattered. Since the banishment, it hadn't been an issue.

Except it was.

Not that either of them seemed to think it was a problem. None of them except Axel. No matter. They were all going to have to find a way to distract themselves for the time being. At least until a solution presented itself.

Just then, Axel's ears tuned in to the sound of a helicopter. *Perfect. Their first guests would be just the distraction he needed.*

It started as a grumble deep inside, but quickly built in strength and intensity until Axel opened his impressive jaws and let out the roar inside until it echoed against the valley walls as the helicopter dipped and flew directly overhead.

"Did you see that?"

Harper had been staring out the window from the moment they'd taken off. She'd never been in a helicopter before and the view was incredible. She whacked Nina on the arm in an effort to get her attention, but she was still intently focused on her phone and frantically tapped a message on the tiny keyboard.

"Nina." Harper shook her sleeve. "Seriously. There are bears out there. Look!"

She pointed again to the ridge and the giant grizzly she'd seen a moment earlier up on his hind legs. Obviously, she couldn't hear anything, but Harper knew the grizzly was roaring. It sent a shiver through her entire body and straight to her core.

Wow, it had been awhile since she'd been laid. The fact that she could find a wild animal—a bear—even slightly arousing was definitely a sign that she needed to scratch an itch. In a very bad way. And that's just what she'd do...as soon as she was done on the mountain with Nina.

Who was *still* on her phone!

"Nina! Seriously. Look at that bear." She pointed out the window where the bear in question had turned and ran back through the woods. As the helicopter flew overhead, the animal almost seemed to keep pace. Harper knew she was having a once-in-a-lifetime experience. To be able to see a grizzly so close up was amazing. And oddly exhilarating. "He's gorgeous!"

"Gorgeous?" That got her friend's attention. "Only you would talk about an animal that way. You're such a horn dog. You seriously need to have sex. With a man," she added and Harper rolled her eyes. Nina leaned across Harper and looked out the window. "You're totally right though. That is a magnificent specimen."

Harper laughed. "Now who's a horn dog?"

"I'm just saying." She shrugged. "Maybe we'll get to see one in person. It is called Grizzly Ridge, after all."

"I hope we don't," Harper said even though she did secretly hope they'd see a bear up close. "They're dangerous and that's not exactly the type of holiday I was hoping to have." In fact, she hadn't been hoping to have the kind of holiday where she was stranded at the top of a mountain in a lodge in the middle of nowhere Montana, either. But beggars couldn't be choosers. And even if it wasn't one of Nina's posh spa assignments, she'd take it. Anything to get away from her life for a bit.

Harper turned to look back at the bear, but she couldn't spot him again. He must have been swallowed up in the forest as the helicopter moved toward the landing pad. It was a good thing anyway. Bears were dangerous. It was probably for the best if he kept his distance.

Read the rest of His to Protect Now!
Buy Direct from the author HERE!

About the Author

Elena Aitken is a USA Today Bestselling Author of more than fifty romance and women's fiction novels. The mother of 'grown up' twins, Elena now lives with her very own mountain man in the heart of the very mountains she writes about. She can often be found with her toes in the lake and a glass of wine in her hand, dreaming up her next book and working on her own happily ever after.

To learn more about Elena:
www.elenaaitken.com
elena@elenaaitken.com